Blissful Lust

The Goddess of Lust, Love and Infatuation: Part Two

Written By

Champagne

P.O. Box 841

Tobyhanna, PA 18466

(973) 348-5067

sspublishingcompany@gmail.com

www.sharsheypublishingcompany.com

Copyright © 2018 Sharon Terry

ISBN: 13: 978-0-9997922-1-6

ISBN: 10: 0-9997922-1-0

Publisher: Shar- Shey Publishing Company LLC

Book Cover Designed by: Dynasty's Visionary Designs

Edited by: ATW Editing

Table of Contents

ACKNOWLEDGMENTS

Thank you my Lord and Savior for the journey.

A special thanks to my parents Shirley & Eddie. My children Khendaijah, Damon, Kristal, Dammond, John, Sharron, Jaquan, and Jermaisha for believing in me.

Oscar, Amy, Brandon, Brianna, Janice, Genesis, and Tykia for encouraging me to push forward.

Thanks to Shar-Shey Publishing, editors, and designers for the crisp editing and stunning book design. Without you, this book would have never found its way to the web or printed books.

CHAPTER ONE

~ The New Adventure ~

"Hey, cousin. It's Reggie. Me and my wife are on our way to your place. We're catching a cab from the airport."

Johnathan replies, "What's up, boy? It's been a minute. I will be waiting for you, Cuz."

Reggie hangs up the phone and proceeds to wave down a cab for him and Heavenly.

"Reggie, you told him I was your wife. What if they don't believe us, or know something is wrong?" Heavenly asks nervously.

Reggie quickly responds, "Listen, baby, you *are* my wife. If you don't believe it, then how will anyone else? Furthermore, stop being nervous. You got to be a grown woman now."

Heavenly smiles at Reggie as he compassionately puts his arm around her. "I know it was all worth it and besides, wife sounds good," Heavenly says.

Reggie looks at Heavenly with a smile on his face because he knows his plan is going to go more smoothly than expected. He turns his head and looks out the window as a sense of peace overcomes him.

Heavenly is focused straight ahead looking at the sites of the new city as she replays Reggie's words in her mind. "Listen, baby, you are my wife." Those words melt her heart and make her want to move forward with her plan to keep Reggie around for life.

The cab pulls up to Johnathan's home. They exit the car to go up to the door and knock. Johnathan meets them at the door. "Welcome, cousin Reggie. Boy, you look good and your wife is beautiful." He holds out his hand to give Heavenly a proper greeting as he says, "I truly apologize for being rude. I didn't catch your name, lovely lady."

Heavenly accepts his extended hand. "My name is Heavenly."

He gestures for them to come in and closes the door behind them. Heavenly drops her purse and looks around because she is amazed at the beauty of Johnathan's home. She is intrigued by the beautiful lion statues that sit in the walkway and the stairwell equipped with an antique spiral handrail with detailed carvings.

"You can come this way, Heavenly. I will show you where you will be sleeping," Johnathan says. He walks Heavenly to the room and then goes to the kitchen where Reggie awaits. "Yo, she is fine. How you get that? That ain't the chick you brought the last time. Man, that other chick wore so much makeup I thought she was coming to do a commercial," Johnathan says with a chuckle.

Reggie responds with a smile on his face. "Dude, lower your voice. Furthermore, boy, you're talking about Lisa, my son's mother. So chill with the corny jokes. You ain't funny. Stop gawking over my wife and get you one, my dude."

Johnathan looks at Reggie, amused by what he just said. "Man, I ain't mess with a chick that I don't have to offer alcohol and baby wipes because of all that damn makeup. Don't get it twisted. I get chicks, my dude. I'm just amused to see some natural beauty, so I hope you don't think I want her. But you are lucky. She got any sisters?"

Reggie replies sarcastically, "I guess I am lucky, but her sister is young. So you're out of luck, my boy. Carry on with the chicks you been messing with."

"Well you better keep her bad and boujee ass happy, because these dudes going to be on her. But for real thought, Bra, she fine as hell," Johnathan says.

Reggie shakes his head. "Man, there's more to it than you know. I will definitely fill you in later, but for now I need you to find me a house so we can get settled. It looks like we're going to be here for a while. Yo, you still a real estate agent? What can you do for me?"

"I have my own company," Johnathan says. "I'm a broker. You need at least ten stacks to even talk to me, Bra. Even then, that will get you a decent house, but nothing fancy. Your mortgage may still be sort of high because of the low down payment, unless I go to the city auction and get you a fixer upper. I don't have any clients looking to sell right now. Give me at least a week to see which one would be your best option. Meanwhile, you and your wife can stay here."

"Damn, you just said a lot of shit that I don't even understand," Reggie says. "Just let me know what you can do. Ten stacks ain't nothing. Let me go check on my wife. We'll chat it up later." Reggie slaps Johnathan up, then leaves the kitchen and heads toward the room to check on Heavenly.

"Hey, baby, what you doing?" Reggie says as he enters the room with a smile.

Heavenly responds with a smile. "Hey, I thought you were not coming in here; you left me by myself for so long."

Reggie walks up to Heavenly, grabs her face, and says, "I will never leave you for long, but there will always be business I need to handle. So please just be patient with me." He gently kisses her lips, but she tenses up and pulls away.

"Baby, I want a different life here. I don't want anything to remind me of back home. I need to go back to school and get my GED. I want to go to the seminary to get my pastoral degree, and my husband can't be a known drug dealer."

"Heavenly, I will invest my money into legit businesses, and my cousin Johnathan will help me do just that. I'm ready for a change as well. I got your back in whatever you would like to do. Give me a little time to get things in order."

5

Heavenly looks at Reggie as if she wants to believe him, but it's too early to know if he is telling the truth. She sits on the bed and looks at Reggie as she says, "I will try to trust what you tell me, but I don't trust the thoughts you *haven't* told me."

Reggie walks over, sits next to Heavenly, and stares into her eyes. "I can't promise you that I will be perfect, but I will promise you I'm going to keep you happy and content." He suddenly breaks the stare and says, "Enough of that stuff. I need to get in the shower and get some rest. We have a lot of things to do." Reggie gathers his clothes and heads to the shower.

Heavenly lies on the bed in a fetal position thinking of all the things that have transpired, wondering if her life will ever be normal again. She begins to envision the whole scene of her father lying on the bed and her mother begging for him to respond. Reggie always reminds her of her father and there is a connection she feels to him because of that familiar feeling. Suddenly, a tear drops down her cheek as she says, "Lord, you said you would not forsake me, but I feel alone."

She jumps quickly to her feet when she thinks she hears a voice say, "I am here." Emotions of fear and confusion overcome her. Is it her own thoughts, an illusion of her own mind, or is God really talking to her? As she looks around the room frantically, she notices no one is there. She falls to her knees to pray. With tears in her eyes, she looks up to the sky and maintains her silence as she closes her eyes again.

*****

Theresa drops the phone and says, "Oh my God, Christine. Heavenly is with Reggie. I'm sorry. I don't know how this happened, but I know they left town. We can't call anyone. This will expose us all."

"What? My baby is with Reggie? The one you want to kill," Christine exclaims hysterically. "And he knows you want to kill him, right?" She starts yelling and banging on the table. "If he does anything to my baby, I will kill you and that damn ego personally." She looks at Theresa as tears fall down her face, and then she walks away.

Theresa follows Christine. "I never meant for it to go this far. I will get her back unharmed. We just can't put the law into this right now. I'll call Low and see what kind of options I have, or how close he is to finding them."

Christine turns to address Theresa's heartless response. "You see, this is the problem – I always let you fix things and you make more of a mess instead of fixing it. If you would have waited and let everything play out instead of threatening Reggie, my child would be here right now. I let you turn me against the man I truly loved and now I'm at risk of losing my daughter too. This has to stop somewhere, Theresa. You can't fix everything with murder. I still love Julian and these are still our children. If you really love me as your sister, get my daughter here safely so I can move on and fix the rest of this shitty-ass thing called my life." Christine gives Theresa a stern look before walking past her to check on Lindsey and Mark.

*****

"Mark, did you hear what Mom and Aunt Theresa were talking about?" Lindsey asks.

"I covered my ears," Mark replies. "It's too much shouting. Why is everyone so mad at each other? You're not mad at me, are you?"

Lindsey holds Mark as she says, "No. I am not mad at you. We have to find out where Heavenly is. Mom just said that Aunt Theresa's always murdering people. Do you think she killed Heavenly because they don't like each other?"

Mark looks at Lindsey sadly. "Heavenly is not dead. We must pray because she will always be with us. And Dad too. You are scaring me, Lindsey. I just want to go to bed."

They suddenly hear footsteps coming up the stairs, so Mark gets in the bed and Lindsey pretends she is tucking him in. The door opens and they hear a voice say, "Hey, you two. I was coming to check on you. Did you shower?"

Both Lindsey and Mark reply softly in unison, "Yes."

"Well, that's great to hear. I thought I was going to have to force you to take a shower. I am glad you are tucking your brother in. Say your prayers and go to bed. Lindsey, you will continue to sleep in the family room," Christine says. She begins to walk away and leave the two children so they can pray in peace.

Christine stops suddenly in her tracks when Lindsey asks, "Mom, sorry to bother you, but has Heavenly called or come home yet?"

Christine replies, "She did call. She said hello and she loves you guys, but she has gone to stay with a friend for a while."

"Okay, Mom. I'm glad you talked to her, but she doesn't want to speak to us?" Lindsey asks.

Christine looks away. She hates lying to her children, but she doesn't want them to worry about Heavenly, so she says, "She is a little upset and just wanted us to know she is okay."

Lindsey smiles at her mom. "Okay, Mom. If she calls back, me and Mark would like to talk to her."

Christine nods her head to say yes and heads out the door. Lindsey waits until she doesn't hear any more footsteps before she closes the door. After she hears her mom go down the stairs, she says, "Mark, Mom is lying to us. Heavenly would have asked to speak to us, and anyway, what friends does she have besides Lorenzo? She can't live with Lorenzo; he lives with his parents."

"Lindsey, I'm scared," Mark replies. "I don't think Mom is lying. She just doesn't want us to be mad at Heavenly for leaving us."

Lindsey grabs Mark by his cheeks and looks him directly in his eyes. "Mark, trust me. Something is very wrong. Heavenly wouldn't just leave us and not say anything."

"Just pray and she'll be back. You'll see! God has many powers. Heavenly told me that," he says.

Lindsey tucks Mark in, closes the door, and heads downstairs to the family room. As she's walking down the stairs, she sees her aunt Theresa in the dining room drinking her cognac. She hears her mother say in a loud and distressed voice, "Lord, I know I have sinned, but please don't forsake my children. Please forgive me. Don't punish them for my falling short. I have broken many commandments, but they have not broken any."

Lindsey slowly approaches the family room, unnoticed by her aunt Theresa or her mother. She stands in the doorway and stares in disbelief at her mother praying. It's been so long since she's seen her mother pray. "God has not forsaken us. He is always with us and he is with you too," Lindsey says.

Christine stops in the middle of her prayer and looks at Lindsey. "I know God is with is, but I want to make sure my children are protected. I asked him to forgive me so you all won't suffer. We are descendants – relatives – of Adam who brought sin upon us, but Jesus Christ brought love and forgiveness. I don't want you all suffering for my sins." She grabs Lindsey and hugs her tight. The room is silent. Christine

11

kisses her daughter's forehead and then says, "Let's go to bed and have a better day tomorrow. I love you."

"I love you too, Mommy," Lindsey says. They both pull back the covers and get into the bed for a night of rest.

*****

Theresa is sitting at the table trying to figure out what to do as she sips on her comfort. The words that Christine said to her have been on her mind since their argument. She doesn't know what else to do because making people disappear has always been her best option. Now her niece is with Reggie somewhere, and she doesn't know where or why she even left with Reggie. Julian is dead as they had planned, and now Christine seems unstable. There is no telling when she may fold. Theresa has to keep it together because she doesn't want to harm her own family. What they did to the kids' father was enough to traumatize them for life. She picks up the phone to make a call, but she hesitates and places it back on the table.

*****

"You can go take a shower now. It was such a relief," Reggie says. Heavenly is still lying there in a daze, lost in her thoughts. "Heavenly," Reggie says loudly.

She jumps at the sound of her name. "Yes, I heard you and I'm going now to take a shower. I really need to clear my mind." She looks at Reggie, becoming agitated. He doesn't notice her because his full attention is on the television. Heavenly gathers the clothes he left out for her and heads to the shower. She stops in the doorway of the bathroom and she stares at Reggie for a long time, her thoughts increasingly lustful. Her mind wanders as she says, "Oh my, it's getting really hot in here. I guess I will cool off in the shower."

Reggie never responds to Heavenly's comment. She undresses and gets into the shower, only to notice the same hot flash has come upon her again. She doesn't understand why she is suddenly so hot because water is only lukewarm. Every time she thinks of Reggie, she becomes hotter and gets a tingling feeling between her thighs. Heavenly doesn't understand what's going on. It's a good, but weird feeling.

CHAPTER TWO

~ The Unknown ~

Reggie picks up the phone to make a phone call. "Yo, my dude. Is everything good there?"

"I know all our people are safe for now. Where the hell are you?" the voice on the other end of the phone says.

"You know I can't tell you that, but just know that I am good, my dude. Have you heard nothing? It's actually been quiet," Reggie says.

"Those dudes from around the way took over our hood, and yeah somebody said ole girl's niece was missing. Yo, the queen actually came out asking questions by herself. I didn't even know the little young chick. I just know you were kicking it with her."

Reggie quickly says, "That's crazy. She must be serious about finding her niece. I haven't seen that chick since that day at the house, but thanks for keeping me informed. I will touch base with you real soon. Keep your head up, my dude." Reggie hangs up the phone, sits on the bed, and replays the conversation that he just had with his friend.

*****

Heavenly lathers her sponge with body wash as she starts to think about her life with Reggie. She thinks about how handsome and muscular he is, and that tingling feeling comes between her legs this time. She is feeling hot and sweaty, but doesn't understand why she feels that way every time she thinks of Reggie. Heavenly says aloud to herself, "Maybe I'm getting sick from traveling to another state, and from the weather being different."

She brushes off her feelings and begins to wash her body, drifting into her thoughts again. Now she is visualizing her father lying on the bed with blood everywhere, as her mother tried to awaken him in his last minutes. Heavenly starts breathing heavily and feeling lightheaded. She seems to be confused as to where she is, so she closes her eyes tightly and slides to the floor for comfort. She beings to cry and pray because she feels separated from her current presence. Through the cries of prayer, she opens her eyes and everything is suddenly back to normal. Heavenly is lying at the bottom of the tub, feeling confused and disturbed as the water from the shower falls upon her body. Not knowing what just happened, she shakes it off and continues with her shower. Those feelings had come upon Heavenly in the past, but she doesn't know what triggers them. All she knows is that it only happens when she is in the shower.

*****

Theresa leaves the house to go out looking for Heavenly after everyone else has gone to bed for the night. She hates to see Christine so upset and she wants to fix things for her sister. She sees a few guys hanging around the corner and stops to speak with them. She holds a picture of Heavenly in her hand as she asks, "What's up? Have you seen her around here or anywhere?"

One of the guys responds, "Yo, who you? The police? We don't know shit. You better get the fuck from around here with all of that."

Theresa looks him in his eyes as she grabs her piece and says, "I see your little ass don't know who you are talking to. I will waste you right here, but you are not worth my time. Damn worker bee."

She shoves the barrel of the gun firmly into his temple until she hears a voice say, "Queen, he truly meant no disrespect. Not everyone knows who you are. Just let him go and he will apologize, if that's okay with you."

"You must want to die, motherfucker. Don't ever interrupt me," she replies angrily. She looks over at the other young boy and she relaxes her hand off the trigger. "Now, I'm going to ask again: have you seen or do you know her?"

"Yes, that's Heavenly. No one has seen her or talked to her since her Pops got shot," the young man replies.

"How do you know her?" she asks.

"We have been best friends since we were kids."

Theresa takes a closer look at the young man. "Lorenzo, is that you? You have grown since I last seen you." Lorenzo shakes his head in relief as he comes closer to greet Theresa. She puts her piece away and gives him a hug. "So, if you haven't seen Heavenly, have you seen Reggie or his crew around?"

"He hasn't been around either," Lorenzo says. "The dudes around the corner took over the spot, but if I see any of them I will let them know you're looking for them." Lorenzo doesn't know the intent of her questions, but he knows that it doesn't sound good for Reggie. He's aware of how much Heavenly admires Reggie. Heavenly trusted Reggie more than she did Lorenzo. If she's missing, did he kidnap her? Or is she now in a relationship with Reggie and decided to run off with him?

Theresa quickly replies, "No. Don't tell no one I was even around here. Take my number and if you see her, call me immediately. Oh and by the way, why you hang with this dude and he doesn't even know whose hood he's really in? I will let him be great this time, but never make that mistake again, Lorenzo."

She walks away, gets in her car, and pulls off. She has been out looking for Reggie and Heavenly for a while. Theresa is starting to get the idea that she has not given Reggie enough credit. He has outsmarted her for once. Now she needs to see if he or Heavenly have left a paper trail. She will check that on her office computer. Being a business woman in real estate gives her access to personal information. She can look up assets and previous addresses as well as any current ones. For now, she heads home to get some rest. First thing tomorrow, she will use Reggie's government identity and find out who he really is.

*****

Heavenly dries off, puts on her clothes, and heads to the room. She feels so out of place right now. The house is really nice and spacious. She's with Reggie as planned, but this is unfamiliar to her. She has no underwear, hair supplies, or clean socks. It's just not home. She is starting to have second thoughts about her actions, but it was her choice. She enters the room where Reggie is watching TV and once again, he doesn't notice her presence. She stares at him as she asks, "Do you think we made the right decision? I don't know…why does it feel all wrong now?" She walks toward Reggie and sits on the bed.

He looks up and places his arm around her waist. "I understand you have mixed feelings, but I just gave you what you said you wanted. We're going shopping to get you some new things. We're going to look for our own house and will definitely hit the school you want to go to as well – missionary or whatever."

Heavenly replies with a smile on her face. "It all sounds great and all. I trust you and I really respect your opinion. I just miss my brother and sister. I wish we could go right now. I am more than ready to start school."

Reggie gently touches Heavenly's chin and says, "Relax, baby. I got you. We are going to get some sleep and tomorrow we're going to start our new life." Heavenly leans forward and softly kisses Reggie to thank him.

Reggie is stuck for a few seconds as he tries to comprehend the kiss. "Listen, Heavenly. You are beautiful, but you are not even eighteen years old yet, so I would like it if you don't do that again." He gets up and walks out of the room because he knows his hormones are racing just like Heavenly's, but he feels guilty. She is his daughter's age.

Heavenly sits on the bed feeling rejected, not pretty enough, and disappointed that she moved so quickly. She wants Reggie to want and need her. That is what she is used to. Now she must have him and she plans to make it official for her eighteenth birthday. She will get what she wants one way or another. He needs to know she is not a baby anymore.

*****

When Theresa enters her home, she puts her piece on the table, pours some cognac, and sits at the table. She is trying to figure out how to handle this situation without being messier than she already has been. Obviously, Reggie is smarter than she thought. He and Heavenly cannot have up and disappeared!

She jumps up and goes to her china cabinet where she keeps a list of all her important and well respected contacts. As she looks down the list, she thinks of their professions and how they could help. She stops at the name "Richard Mezz" and she suddenly begins to smile. Richard was attracted to Theresa. She slept with him once, but his obsession with her was a turn off. She knows this is the very connection she needs – he is a private investigator. He knows who she is in the business world, but not the real woman she is outside of business.

She places the paper back in the cabinet and plans on calling him in the morning. This will be a great start and will definitely be helpful in finding Heavenly and Reggie. She knows if she finds Heavenly, she will probably find that snake

Reggie. Theresa calls Low to tell him what the plans are from now on.

"Hello, Low. How have you been?" Theresa asks.

"I have been great, Queen," Low replies. "I been all around town visiting the family, but no one has seen Cousin Reggie."

"I love Cousin Reggie and how well prepared he is, but for now we just got to let him live his life. He will surface sooner or later," Theresa says. "I really appreciate you for checking on him, but I have a good friend that will take over for now. Meet me at the chicken spot tomorrow for dinner. That's the least I can do for all your effort."

Low replies, "I will see you there. I need at least six wings and a waffle."

They both laugh and agree that the meeting will be tomorrow at 7:00 pm. She knows that she has to bring six racks for Low's services. She decides to get the money before she forgets, so she removes six stacks from her safe behind the picture in the dining room. She doesn't want Christine or anyone to know she even keeps a stash in the house. She places the money in her purse and proceeds upstairs to go to bed.

*****

Heavenly wakes up and looks over her shoulder at Reggie. They are in the same bed, but slept far away from each other. She notices that he's still asleep, so she turns on the television to occupy her until he wakes up. As she flips through the channels, she stops at a worldwide channel. Nothing they are broadcasting about is interesting to her, so she is getting ready to turn the channel until she hears, "In the New Orleans murder of Julian Valone...."

Heavenly jumps up to listen to the news more closely. Her heart weakens from what her eyes are witnessing – Lindsey, Mark, and her mother running from reporters. She makes up her mind at that moment. She will be returning home for the trial. Lindsey and Mark have to get away from that monster before they are the next ones dead for their money. Coming up with a plan to get back home without Reggie won't be easy, but she has to find a way.

As Heavenly is lost in her thoughts, Reggie wakes up unnoticed by her. He rolls over and says, "How long have you been up watching that negative information they blind us with?"

Heavenly jumps at the sound of Reggie's voice. "I just turned the TV on to occupy my time until you woke up, but I haven't been up that long."

"Well, turn that shit off," Reggie replies. "Are you ready for the day? We got business to handle."

"Of course I'm ready to go shopping." Heavenly smiles at Reggie as she gets up and gets ready for the day. Reggie leaves the room to go speak with his cousin so he can get some directions to where he will be going.

Reggie knocks on the door to Johnathan's room. "Yo, you up? I need you to tell me where the mall's at and my wife needs to find that missionary school around here."

"I'm up now, motherfucker. Give me a minute or two. I got you." Johnathan, feeling rushed by Reggie, gets up and starts getting ready.

Reggie returns to the room with Heavenly and informs her of the plans. As he is about to enter the room, Heavenly is switching her shirts. He stands in the doorway, staring at her beautiful body.

Heavenly doesn't see him at first, but something overcomes her as she feels someone's presence. She knows this is the start of the game she wants to play with Reggie. She slowly struggles with her shirt, giving him the illusion that it's difficult for her to get it on.

Reggie breaks out of the seductive trance and excuses himself. "I am so sorry. I thought you were already dressed. When you're done, I will be in the kitchen," he says as he turns and walks away. Reggie knows that things like this cannot keep happening because he is not sure how long he can control himself. He had never seen her bare skin before, and now that he has, he really wants to make it official between the two of them.

*****

"Reggie, I found a nice spot for you on the auction website, but there may be a few things that need to be fixed on the house. I will take you to look at the house one day this week. You can use my other car in the garage; it has a GPS system in it." Johnathan leans close to Reggie as he says, "Let me ask you a question, if you don't mind." Reggie nods his head yes and Johnathan says, "What kind of freak is your wife? No disrespect, but she definitely don't seem holy and sanctified. Hell, that's all you mess with, and if she got you to marry her, yup she a big freak!" Johnathan bursts into an uncontrolled chuckle.

With a smirk on his face, Reggie says, "Man, that is very disrespectful, my dude. She's not holy and sanctified, but she is a virgin. I definitely will be her first everything."

Johnathan looks at Reggie in disbelief. "What… She must be a born again virgin, or is that what she's telling you? Because she too damn fine for not one person to have touched that. I mean, even emotionally."

"You are too much for your own good. I do have some things to fill you in about, but later for that, Cuz. Where them keys at?" Reggie asks.

"I know she was a stripper. She just looks seductive, but I know you will keep it real….." Johnathan trails off as Heavenly enters the room.

"Okay, Reggie. I'm all ready to go, and good morning Johnathan," Heavenly says. She looks at the both of them, noticing that they seem surprised to see her.

Reggie breaks the awkward tension as he grabs the keys and waves for Heavenly to follow him.

CHAPTER THREE

~ Snakes in Disguise ~

Andrew lies in his cell, staring at the ceiling and thinking of everything he has gotten himself into with Slim and Christine. He knows he may not get out anytime soon, but he still holds on to the memories of him and Christine. He wishes he could turn back time and stand up as a man. If he'd just stood up to Slim and told him he really loved Christine, it might have gone a little differently. But then he remembers that he fell in love with someone he didn't know at all. The image of finding the identification card removes all the emotions of love. He now feels confused again.

As he thinks more about it, Slim and Christine set him up. Still, he can't help but remember the fact that he loves Christine. The more he thinks about it, the sadder he becomes.

"Do you know who has that yayo? I got a lot on my mind. Please just let me know what I got to do to get some," Andrew says to his cellmate.

"You know that stuff is more expensive in here. You can get $40 worth of commissary for a dime bag," his cellmate replies.

Andrew looks at him as if he has something on his face. He doesn't have any money and no way to get any. "Can you just credit me until I can get in touch with someone in my family? I promise I will pay you back. I'm in need, man," Andrew says.

"Let me talk to my people. I will see what he has to say." The cellmate walks out of the cell to talk to the main person in charge of the whole transaction.

*****

As Slim walks across the mess hall with his breakfast tray, he sets eyes on a few dudes he knows. He walks in their direction. As he approaches the table and greets them, he says, "Man, I was looking around to see who I know from the hood, but I didn't see anybody until now. I am so glad to see a few familiar faces."

One of the guys responds, "Yo, we seen you on TV for smoking ole boy. Man, he was a lame. You could have scared that dude and been good." All the inmates at the table begin to chuckle at the statement.

"Listen, I was threatened by that dude twice," Slim says. "Man, I had to defend myself. Ain't no one just going to keep threatening me and get away with it, so I got him before he got me. These dudes don't be playing nowadays. I don't take threats lightly."

"Yo, you know the news don't tell us all that, but what's up with your cousin? He in here too?" the inmate asks.

Slim replies, "Naw, that sucker ass dude ain't in here with me. I would have done him off by now."

The inmate responds with an amazed look on his face. "That's your family. What the hell you talking about? You were so protective of Andrew. You wouldn't let no one touch him. What happened? You a wild boy."

"He is a sucker for love ass dude, and I am gonna leave it at that," Slim replies. Everyone at the table starts laughing out loud and continues to converse through their meal. Slim sits in a daze as he thinks about how he will he get to Andrew before trial. He knows that Andrew is in love with Christine because he once was in love with her too. He let his feelings go when she really went through with messing with Andrew.

*****

"This is the only option I have right now. Have someone bring in some supplies, specifically pills. We are really scarce on supplies. The chick we had bringing it got busted, so the boss is in the box. I handle all transactions for now, so do you think you can get someone to help out?" Slim's cellmate asks.

"Hell yeah," Slim replies. "Let me call my little chick. She will definitely be with that for real. Next phone call I get, I will let you know when she is coming. When will I be able to get that hook up though?"

The cellmate replies, "I got you now since you have agreed to the contract." He walks out of the cell after giving Andrew his first fix.

Andrew looks around as he happily takes the gift from his cellmate. He knows he doesn't have anyone to call, but all he wants is to get away from reality. Once he notices that no one is around, he puts it on his hand, sniffing the white residue. As he closes his eyes and feels the effect of it heat up his veins, he grabs hold of his bunk bed to catch his fall. He begins to smile, bursting into laughter as he is finally feeling some comfort. All he can think about is his perfect vision of life with Christine, which is the only thing that gives him warm thoughts.

*****

Bonnie gives Theresa a call to check on the children. "Hello, may I speak with Theresa? This is Bonnie from Child Protective Services."

Theresa is just waking up. "Yes, Bonnie. This is me," she mumbles.

"Well, I was calling to check on the children. I noticed Heavenly has not been to school, and apparently she has not been seen for a while. Also, I know their mother was released on bail. Has she been staying with you as well?"

"I am aware that Heavenly has not been to school," Theresa says. "She has been having a hard time dealing with everything, so we let her stay home. She will be eighteen soon and we don't have a lot of influence over her at this time. As far as my sister is concerned, yes she is here until they release the home to her in a few days."

"Christine can be around the children. We only took them because she went to jail, but otherwise she is innocent until proven guilty and that's not our decision. On the other hand, I need to see the children and see how they are doing. By the way, is Heavenly around since she isn't in school? I would love to speak with her to see if there is anything I can do for her," Bonnie says.

Theresa replies, "You can come this evening to see the children, but Heavenly seemed troubled this morning when she was helping her siblings get dressed. She just announced that she was taking a walk. To where, I have no idea. I can let her know you would like to see speak with her alone."

"I will be there around 5:30 pm," Bonnie says. "If she returns before then, please inform her that I need to speak with her."

Theresa and Bonnie hang up after they both agree and say goodbye. Bonnie sits at her desk, confused because based upon what she had witnessed in the little time she spent with the children, Heavenly would never just leave her siblings, angry or not. Heavenly's personality is protective, so she suspects something about Theresa's story isn't right.

*****

Frustrated, Theresa lays the phone down and says aloud, "This little bitch Heavenly is just like her father. She ain't nowhere around, but causing plenty of trouble." She looks over at the time and thinks about her friend Richard, the private investigator. She decides to get up and start her now complicated day. Theresa can smell the aroma of food in the air as she walks down the stairs.

"Christine, are you cooking us breakfast? It smells great," she says as she walks toward the kitchen. There is no response to her calling out to Christine and as she reaches the kitchen, Theresa notices no one is there. She grabs some food that Christine had prepared and heads to the dining area with her glass of orange juice.

She sits back to eat her breakfast, sipping the orange juice after taking bites of her food. She frowns as she says, "I thought orange juice was so nasty without something in it. Oh well, I will need a morning boost anyways." Theresa grabs the cognac and spikes her orange juice. She takes a sip and smiles. She opens the drawer to her china cabinet, goes through the list again, and finds Richard's number. She hesitates to give him a call because she knows he's going to flirt with her like he always does, but she is not at all attracted to him. Picking up her glass, she takes a big gulp of her drink before dialing Richard's number.

Richard picks up the phone and says, "Hello, my love. What gives me the pleasure of hearing your lovely voice this beautiful morning?"

Theresa responds, "Good morning, Richard. I see you are doing well. I am calling because I need a favor. More like I have a job for you."

"That's awesome to hear you need me for something, but what will I get in return for my services?"

"Paid in cash and that will be it, my friend," Theresa replies.

"You know I don't need your money, but I do have an offer for you. If you go on a date with me, I will do the job for you."

"That won't be happening," Theresa replies. "I am involved and I am really into him. It's important I locate my family. We are really worried about his whereabouts. I can and will pay for your services. With that being explained, will you take the job?"

Richard pauses for a few seconds before he finally responds. "Is everything okay with you and your family?"

Theresa puts on a worried and weary voice. "My cousin has been missing for a few weeks and my aunt is worried about him. He has children and I just want to make sure he is alive. I didn't go to the police because he wasn't a saint, if you know what I mean. You won't be in any danger. Just let us know he is alive or could be alive."

Richard replies, "Well I respect you as a very empowered woman of this community and if you need me, I'm your guy. No strings attached. There are a few things I need to start this investigation – name, date of birth, last known address, mother, father, spouse or significant other, and children. If you don't have all the information, we can start with name, alias, date of birth, etc… You can fax me all the information that you gather."

"Thank you so much for helping me and my family," Theresa says. "I will have the information to you by tomorrow afternoon."

Richard says, "Since we have confirmed I am hired, I will send you a contract via your email and it will contain a fee for my services." They both agree and end the conversation

Theresa has a sinister grin on her face as she begins to dial another number. "Hey, my favorite cousin. We are going to have to make that dinner date a little later. Would 9:00 pm be fine?"

Low replies, "Of course, Queen. I'm free whenever you need me."

Theresa replies excitedly, "I got some great news for you about our cousin Reggie. I got a friend of mine looking for him as well, but we will catch up on details at dinner."

*****

"Mommy, where is Heavenly and why are you acting like you don't care?" Lindsey asks. She patiently awaits her mother's response as she looks at Mark to assure him nothing is wrong.

Christine calmly looks in the mirror and responds, "Lindsey, baby, it's not that I don't care. I don't know where she is and if we call the police they may take you and Mark from us. Her birthday is tomorrow and she will be considered an adult, so I can't make her come home. I truly miss her, just like you and Mark. I can't lose you two, so we must hope and pray for her return."

Christine doesn't even look at Lindsey as she's responding. She needs them to really believe that she does miss and love her daughter. Things are so out of order, Christine feels out of place in every aspect of her life. The last couple of weeks have been an emotional disaster for Christine and she needs to clear her head.

She parks the car in front of the school, turns, and looks at Lindsey and Mark. "It's been rough on all of us, but I know we can get through this. Heavenly will be back and we will be a family again." She compassionately stares at her children as she wants them to be comforted by her words. Both of the children stare back at her with confusion and discomfort on their faces.

"Mom, how can we be a family when you don't know where Heavenly is and Daddy is dead?" Lindsey responds.

Christine is caught off guard by Lindsey's reply because she has never spoken to her this way. Christine calmly replies,

"Baby girl, a lot has happened and I can't blame you for being angry, but we will be a family again and I promise you that. Have a great day in school and I love you both."

Lindsey turns her head and attempts to slam the door until she feels a resistance. "Ouch that hurts," Mark says as he attempts to exit behind Lindsey. She hears Mark's subtle cry of pain and turns to comfort him. She grabs his hand as he limps toward the school doors.

Christine waits as she watches them go into the building. After they enter the building, Christine begins to lash out in anger as she pounds on the steering wheel while saying, "I fucking ruined everything I stand for. My husband is dead, my children have been corrupted by all this, and Andrew is in jail. But most of all, my Heavenly is gone."

Christine pulls away from the school and she tries to pull herself together by wiping her face. She wipes her face as she thinks of all the tears she has shed for Julian over the years. Angrily, she begins to talk out loud. "He should have never done me wrong. I was faithful to him and our family before that bitch Charlene came along. He only made me angrier because he couldn't make up his mind. If he would have never lied and kept telling me he loved me, I would have never held on. She could have had him, but he wanted to hold on to me instead of letting me live my life. No, but he wouldn't do that. You wanted me to be alone, all while you played with that tramp. How fucking selfish you were and I still managed to give you my all. You didn't love me. How foolish was I to let my heart control me."

Christine stops at a light and looks in the mirror as she continues to clean her face. She continues to talk to herself. "Motherfucker thought you won. Now you dead, bitch. I didn't deserve to be hurt because I truly loved you and you didn't deserve to die because you loved me. Karma is a bitch, isn't Julian?"

She pulls out her makeup kit in an attempt to fix her face. Suddenly, she is startled by a horn. She looks over and the driver is shaking his head in disbelief. He puts his hand near his temple and twirls it as a way to imply that she's crazy. She throws the makeup in the passenger seat and peels off at a very high speed to catch up to the other driver. Unfortunately, she does not catch up to the driver, so she heads home.

*****

As Theresa sits at her desk, she picks up her phone to a make call. "Hey, it looks like you left in a hurry this morning. Is everything okay?"

Christine replies, "I was running behind, but what can I help you with, girl?"

"I didn't sleep with you last night, so tone it down. Have you spoken with the insurance company? I really think this damn CPS worker is going to be a problem. She's coming by today and she wants to see Heavenly!"

Christine shakes her head in disbelief. "This is entirely too much shit! I talked to the insurance agent and they will be releasing the check in a few days, but I don't need nothing or no one messing this up. I mean, I wish I did sleep with someone last night, but one's dead and the other's in jail. By the way, what the hell will I tell this woman? We both look irresponsible at this point. Furthermore, you are the damn genius. Why the fuck you asking or telling me anything?"

Theresa looks at the phone and chuckles. "Calm the fuck down. Ain't nobody put no gun to your head. Besides, just talk to your kids and let them know she is coming. That way, they won't say anything out of line. Do you think your weak ass can take care of that?"

Christine replies sarcastically, "Sure, so I have a choice." She hangs up the phone, ending their conversation. She continues to drive until she pulls up in front of her house.

Christine has never felt this way before. She closes her eyes and beings to pray. To her surprise, the negative feelings begin to go away. As she opens her eyes, she stares directly at the house as a mass of tears steadily flow down her face. Looking through her blurry vision, all she can see is a mirage of Julian outside playing with the children. While holding her head in her hands, she gives out a big scream, "Why? I don't know if I am going crazy, but I thought I wanted you dead. Now I feel like a big part of me has died. I can't tell anyone that I made a mistake and reacted out of anger because I murdered us, our family."

Christine continues to cry profusely for few minutes until she remembers why all this happened in the first place. "Why am I crying? He never cared about us when he was alive – cheating, lying, only coming around when him and his bitch had problems, or when he needed peace from all the turmoil he caused. Yeah, my heart, my children, all jeopardized for his peace. He got peace now. Rest in peace, motherfucker." She fixes her makeup again and pulls off to go to Theresa's house.

*****

Theresa is at her office taking care of some paperwork for some homes she is selling. She is getting ready to close her computer as she thinks of Reggie. She thinks of Reggie's girlfriend and his daughter, who she met at one of their unannounced meetings. She looks up Reggie's information using his last known address. As she sits in front of the computer with a smile on her face, she picks up the phone to call Richard instead of faxing or emailing him. Unfortunately, Richard doesn't answer and the call goes to voicemail, so she leaves a message.

"Hello, Richard. This is Theresa. I received your contract and will sign and email it back to you later today. I have some of that information for you, pertaining to my cousin. Well, his name is Reggie – Reginald. He has a daughter and a son that are in this area, but I'm not sure where they are located. I have an old address for them and also a female who was listed as living there. I'm not sure where his mother or father is because we haven't spoken to them in years. Well, that's another story. Just call me if you get any leads. I will include all the information in the email as well. Thank you so much for helping me and I hope to hear from you soon." Theresa looks at the time and realizes she has to get home and get ready for Bonnie to come by.

*****

Christine's head is on overload as she continues to sip on her glass. She begins to become extremely angry at herself and anyone who has something to do with the way her life is going right now. Her anger is focused more toward Theresa because she would have never thought of this evil shit on her own. She had always depended on Theresa to help her get revenge on anyone. She realizes her whole life has been a disaster because she has always been a follower and not a leader. Now she wants to take control of her own life, but she doesn't know how to. Christine becomes distracted from her thoughts when she hears someone coming in the house.

Theresa walks in the house and yells, "Christine, where are you?"

Christine replies, "I am in the fucking kitchen."

Theresa starts walking toward the kitchen as she says, "What is wrong with you?"

She is rudely interrupted by Christine. "I'm drinking. My life is a damn mess and you – your evil ass is to blame!"

Theresa looks at Christine. "Why are you drinking? You have to pick up the kids and furthermore, don't fucking cry now! You wanted revenge, you got it. Deal with it, Sweetie."

Christine jumps up and staggers toward Theresa with her hand to the side. With a grin on her face, she says, "You are using your manipulation on me again and it won't work. I think I need to have the plan for once." She slowly brings her hand up in the air as she reveals the knife, looks at Theresa in the eyes, and says, "I don't know who I wanna kill first – me or your evil ass."

Theresa ignores her. She smiles and says, "I think you should start with yourself because, bitch, I been dead for a long time. So go ahead. Do me and many others the big favor."

Christine holds the knife in the air. She can't bring herself to swing it.

"Just as I thought. The perfect church girl can't deal with the real world." Theresa kisses Christine on the cheek and starts to walks away. "Get yourself together. The CPS worker will be here soon. Clean up this mess and yourself. I'm going to get the kids." She walks out the door and slams it aggressively. Christine drops the knife to the floor and slowly sits in the chair to get her thoughts together.

CHAPTER FOUR

~ Loyalty ~

"Heavenly, you know I want to give you the world, being that you're my wife in this new chapter of our life. We have to be cautious about being fancy because we don't want too much attention. I'm gonna give you this stack and you do what you can with it," Reggie says as he hands Heavenly the money.

Heavenly looks seductively at Reggie and says, "Is this what husbands do for their wives? Hell, I would be mad too if someone tries to overstep their boundaries."

Reggie looks out of the corner of his eye at Heavenly and ignores her comment as he continues to drive. Heavenly notices his silence and says, "My birthday is tomorrow. What will we be doing?"

Reggie replies, "I will have something big planned for your big eighteenth birthday. Just relax and make sure you get that grown and sexy outfit for tomorrow."

Heavenly smiles. "It's already done." Heavenly's mind has wandered into thinking about how she will seduce Reggie for her birthday. She needs to keep him in her life because the only man she has ever loved is dead.

They have arrived at the mall and Reggie tells Heavenly to go in and shop. He will wait for her in the car. Heavenly reaches over, hugs him, and kisses him on the cheek. She heads into the mall.

Reggie watches as Heavenly walks in to make sure she is gone before he makes a phone call. "Hello," says Reggie.

"Hey, baby. What's up?" Lisa, Reggie's girlfriend, replies.

"How are you and Junior? Has Sadie gotten down there yet?" Reggie asks.

Lisa replies, "You asking all these questions, but yes she is here and we are fine. We are worried about you. No calls, texts, or anything. What the fuck is really going on?"

"Baby, are you going to talk crazy on this phone?"

"I'm listening, baby. I didn't know what to think – whether you were dead or alive!"

"You are going to be there for a while, baby. I still have some things to clear up and it's not safe. It's getting real intense right now. How are you on cash?" he asks.

Lisa replies, "Okay, but we miss you and it's hard without you here with us."

"I promise to at least text you and keep you at peace. Tell the kids I love them and I will be with all of ya'll real soon. I love you and hold the kids down until I get there." He blows kisses through the phone before he hangs up.

He dials another number as he looks around to make sure Heavenly is not approaching unannounced. "Hello, my beautiful queen," Reggie says with a smile on his face.

Theresa replies, "A peasant like you don't have any right to call me queen. What the fuck you want, motherfucker?"

"No, I'm not running shit, but I am in charge of this whole shit," Reggie says. "It's cool you don't care. I'll just fuck the little bitch and send the video to your sister. How would she feel seeing her daughter get dicked down by an anaconda and actually enjoying it? Don't you think that could be very nerve wrecking for the church girl?"

"Go ahead. I hope she enjoys the scene. I will just keep her calm until I find you and your family. Sodomy can be painful for a male or female. So test me, Reggie. I will wipe out generation after generation until none of you exist. Now we both know Cousin Low loves me enough to make anything and everybody disappear, but the thing is, you don't know if he is your neighbor or the dude off the block. So my precious Reggie, I am not worried. Put up or shut up." Theresa hangs up the phone because she knows that Reggie is not that stupid to cross the line.

Reggie looks at the phone in disbelief as he screams, "Tonight I'm going to fuck this bitch. She gonna test my word. That's all a man got. Game on from here. I want to kill this little bitch and throw her ass on the step. She's threatening my family; this bitch done lost her mind." He puts his hands on his head as he gathers his thoughts.

He picks up the phone and dials another number. "Yo, Cuz. I need a really nice hotel to go to tonight. Did you get shit situated with the house? I need to be in it this week."

Johnathan replies, "Damn, Cuz. You just rambling on like a female. Listen, if you can put at least $10,000 down, which is ten percent of actual cost, I will waive my fees, but you will need to fix a few things. That's why the down payment is low. It's an 'as is' purchase, but why are you in such a rush to get this house?"

"I told you I will fill you in later," Reggie says. "Just get that done. I will see you in the morning. I'm about to go in this mall, grab me a few things, and go to the hotel. Text me that information and don't forget the hotel." He hangs up the phone. He heads into the mall as he dials Heavenly's number. "Baby, where you at? I'm coming in."

Heavenly replies, "I'm in Macy's. Where are you?"

"I'm just passing the food court. I'm coming to Macy's. Stay there." Reggie walks through the mall to go meet Heavenly.

*****

Johnathan picks up the phone. "Hello, I have a buyer right now. They will take the house as it is and will have the down payment tomorrow. Do you already have the code inspection?"

The owner replies, "Yes, we had that done when we decided to put the house on the market. I do have the paperwork. So what time would you like to meet to discuss this matter?"

"9:00 am tomorrow would be a great time, if that works for you."

"Great, I will see you then."

*****

Reggie walks around the store looking for Heavenly. When he spots her talking to a clerk, she doesn't even notice him. He sneaks up behind her, grabbing her waist and pulling her close to him. He hugs her neck.

Heavenly instantly smiles and says, "You scared me, but you feel good that close to me." Reggie lets Heavenly go. She turns and they go into a deep trance as they look at each other.

"I will be over here if you need something," the clerk says. They both suddenly break the stare and Heavenly continues to get the clerk's assistance.

Reggie walks off to see what he can purchase as he says, "I hope you grab something nice. I got a surprise for you tonight."

Heavenly looks at Reggie with a big, beautiful smile on her face. She is thinking to herself that Reggie is not the only one with a surprise.

Reggie walks over to the men's section, looking for something casual to wear to dinner. While looking at himself in the mirror, he tries on a button-up to go under his blazer. "This shirt is perfect." He heads over to the area with cologne; this is one accessory he knows that most women like and can't resist. He takes a sniff of a few expensive colognes until he finds the one that he likes the most. "I will take this one along with these items," Reggie says to the clerk.

"Great choice. This is very popular with the ladies. Are you going on a date with a special someone?" the clerk asks.

"Yes, she is special. She means more to me than she knows," Reggie says with a smile on his face. The cashier rings him out as Reggie looks around to locate Heavenly. He doesn't see Heavenly anywhere, so he decides to make the hotel reservation as he is cashing out.

The cashier, who has been eavesdropping on his conversation, says, "I guess she *is* a special lady, if you're making a reservation at that hotel." The cashier turns and, noticing another customer, tends to them.

Reggie finishes making hotel reservations and walks off to find Heavenly. "Now that all the reservations are made, I gotta find this damn girl."

*****

Heavenly picks up her phone and calls Reggie. "Hey, baby. Where are you? I walked around the store looking for you, but I'm in the hallway in front of the store."

Reggie replies, "I'm on my way now. Stay right there." He hangs up and walks quickly toward the exit so Heavenly doesn't decide to go to another store. He greets her and they start walking toward the exit of the mall. Reggie comes to an abrupt stop and looks at Heavenly. He smiles while gently biting his bottom lip. "Did you get that grown and sexy outfit for your husband?"

Heavenly smiles softly. "Of course I did, my love." She walks in front of Reggie, knowing he will size her up.

He does just that, but all he can think of is making that video to send to Christine. The problem is how will he get her mother's number? Reggie puts the address to the hotel Johnathan had sent him in the GPS.

Heavenly notices the address doesn't look familiar, so she questions their destination. "Baby, where are we going? Because that's not Johnathan's address. We don't know much about this town, so I'm confused."

"Relax. I got a hotel room for us so it can be a special day, alone just us two. Are you okay with that, girl?"

Heavenly sits back and relaxes. "Hell yeah. Boy, I'm good with all of that."

Reggie reaches over to grab her hand, making her feel comfortable before he says, "I think you should call your mother and siblings. Just let them know you're good."

Heavenly looks at Reggie strangely. "I thought you said they could trace us."

"Well, you know they are going to be thinking about you at midnight. It's your birthday. Besides, you can use my phone and I will just get rid of yours. Don't worry. Just don't stay on the phone too long – matter of fact, dial it private. Does that make sense, or sound like something you want to do?"

Heavenly has a big smile on her face when she says, "I really do need to hear all their voices. I know Lindsey is going to ask a lot of questions, but Mark may be really quiet." She turns and looks out the window. She feels that Reggie really cares and wants to see her happy. He knows how much she loves her siblings.

They pull into the hotel parking lot as Reggie finds a parking space. He walks into the hotel and approaches the desk to check in. "I called to reserve the penthouse for tonight. Lankfort is the last name."

The desk clerk looks up his name in the computer and begins the process of checking in. Heavenly looks down at her phone and wants to call her siblings right now, but she knows they should be on their way home from school. She shakes off the thought and decides to take Reggie's advice and wait to call. She looks up and sees if Reggie is coming and she notices he is walking toward the car. She instantly exits the car, opens the back door, and begins to look through the bags to find which ones she is going to take with her. They grab the bags and head into the hotel room.

As they get off the elevator, Heavenly looks around in pure amazement. She has never been to a really nice hotel before. "This is so beautiful. Is this floor just for us? I don't see any other rooms on this floor."

Reggie replies with a smirk on his face. "Yes, baby. I wanted you to wake up to a beautiful view. Anything for my wife on her special day."

Heavenly comes closer to him. As she looks him directly in his eyes, she says seductively, "Thank you. It means so much to me and you mean a lot to me as well."

Reggie looks at Heavenly. "You mean more to me. Let's call your mother and get our afternoon started."

Heavenly looks at Reggie with her phone in his hand, but she hesitates to reach for it. She goes through her contacts and comes to her mother's name and number. As she takes a deep breath, she presses the call button. Reggie comes behind her and holds her close.

"Hello," Christine says.

Heavenly hesitates to respond at first. She finally says, "Hello, Momma."

Christine replies instantly, "Baby, is that you? Thank God. Where are you? Are you okay?"

"I'm fine, Mom. I just needed to get away."

"We miss you, and your birthday is tomorrow. Are you going to come home and celebrate with us? Why did you leave? How can we fix this? The CPS lady is snooping around. You don't want them to take your brother and sister, do you?"

Heavenly sits on the phone, patiently waiting for Christine to stop talking. She has no emotional reaction to the things that her mother is saying, or her mother's supposed concern about her life. "No, Mom. I don't want them taken from you, but I can't come back right now. I need to clear my mind. Can I speak with Lindsey and Mark?"

Christine replies, "How did it get to this point, baby? Just come home and talk to me." She waves at Lindsey and Mark to come to her as she looks to see where Theresa could be. She doesn't want her to know that Heavenly is calling. She whispers to the children that Heavenly is on the phone. The children get excited and want to speak to their sister. She warns them to calm down before Theresa becomes alarmed and comes into the kitchen.

Heavenly waits for one of her siblings to get on the phone. She raises her voice and says, "Mom, I don't have long, but I want to speak to Lindsey and Mark."

Christine looks at Lindsey and Mark with disappointment on her face because she knows Heavenly doesn't want to speak with her, so she passes the phone to Mark. He snatches the phone out of his mother's hand and says, "Hi, sister."

"How have you been? I miss you," Heavenly says.

Mark responds with a very sad tone in his voice, "I miss you too, but why won't you come home?"

"Mark, I promise you will see me soon. You be good and listen to Mommy and Lindsey. I will have a surprise for you when I come back home. We will all be together again. I love you." Heavenly awaits Mark reply.

There is a long awkward silence before he says, "Okay." He passes the phone to Lindsey and walks quietly into the other room.

"Hello. I miss you so much. Where are you? Why did you leave us?" Lindsey rambles on, awaiting Heavenly's answers.

Heavenly brushes her fingers through her hair in distress. "I'm fine. I will come to see you soon."

Lindsey responds angrily, "You left us here with them. I never been away from you on your birthday. I can't wait to see you. When are you coming? Tomorrow?"

"I'm sorry you are upset, but please forgive me. I love you. Put Mom back on the phone," Heavenly says.

Lindsey throws the phone at Christine and walks away. She is not satisfied with Heavenly's response. Heavenly looks over her shoulder and Reggie signals her to hurry up and get off the call. "Well, Christine, please do better with Mark and Lindsey than you did with me. Don't try to contact me after this because this phone will be off."

Christine tries to say a few words to Heavenly, but she has already disconnected the call. Heavenly looks at Reggie as he comes over to comfort her.

"I will dispose of this phone," Reggie says. "I know it was a very hard phone call to make, but you should get in the shower and I will come in to wash you up – help you relax."

Heavenly takes her clothes and heads to the shower while Reggie looks around to see where he will set up the phone so he can record the video.

CHAPTER FIVE

~ Establishment ~

Andrew looks back at the other people in the line, feeling the pressure to make a phone call. He picks up the receiver and dials Christine's number. When she picks up and accepts the call, Andrew says, "Hello, I know we should not be talking, but I needed to hear your voice at least one time. I would really like for you to come see me. I miss you so much."

There is complete silence before Christine responds. "Don't call my damn phone. Call my lawyer if you want to talk to me, stupid motherfucker." She hangs up the phone and instantly becomes agitated. She knows they were all told by the lawyers not to have contact with any of the other defendants.

Andrew stands with the receiver still in his hand, but he continues the conversation as if Christine is still on the phone. He is confused by Christine's response, but he has to make it look good because he wants to ensure his supply keeps coming.

Now he knows that it is getting real and it's every man for himself. He finally hangs up the phone and heads back to his cell to speak with his cellmate.

"I set that up with ole girl, but she won't make it for a couple of weeks. Is that cool?"

The cellmate responds, "As long as you have my collateral. I trust you, my dude. If you decide to cross me, trust you will not live to hear these words again."

Andrew agrees with his cellmate and they have an official handshake to secure the contract.

*****

Slim finishes his food and walks to his cell. On the way, he decides to have a conversation with another inmate. "Yo, this dude Andrew is a real threat to my freedom. If he sides with this chick, I am never going to get out of here."

"Well, what are you going to do about it?" the inmate asks. "I mean, either way you are going to get time."

"I definitely got to do something and I gotta get to it right now," Slim replies. They both look at each other.

The inmate knows Slim is very serious about his statement. "Man, you know these streets don't have no love for no one. I respect your decision because it's you or him, my dude, family or not," the inmate says.

They slap each other up and walk in opposite directions. Slim walks toward the guard to ask a question. "When can I make a phone call? I really need to speak to my family, especially my mom."

The guard assures Slim that he will take him to make the call shortly. The guard gestures for the other guard to come his way. He informs the guard of his plans to take Slim to use the phone.

Slim picks up the phone and dials his mother's number. The phone rings. A big, bright smile comes upon his face as he hears his mother's voice. "Hello, Mom. How are you doing?"

"Hello, Son. I am okay, but how are you?"

"I'm doing so much better now that I've heard your voice. I am so sorry, Mom, for disappointing you. I always wanted to make life easier for you and Charlene, but it seems I only mess it up." A tear drops down his face as he expresses his desire to give them a better life.

His mother responds gracefully. "Son, pray. God still loves you and He will never forsake you. I love you and never stop loving you, but Son, I must tell you some disturbing news. Charlene is in the hospital for attempted suicide and she is four months pregnant. The baby is fine so far and she is in an induced coma to save both of their lives. I have been up there a few times…."

Slim interrupts with a loud roar of sorrow as he drops the phone and falls to the ground on his knees. "Charlene. No, not Charlene. Charlene," he screams.

The guards rush to his aid, ready to assist him if he is in need of any medical attention. As he continues to repeatedly spurt out, "Charlene, not Charlene again," the guards ask questions to see how can they help

"Are you having any pain, Sir?"

Slim shakes his head in response. "No."

"Is Charlene your mother, girlfriend, or close relative?" the guard asks.

Slim pulls himself slowly to his knees and says, "It's my baby sister. She is in a coma and four months pregnant. What have I done to my sister?"

Meanwhile, on the other end of the phone, his mother is listening to her son fall apart from the disappointing news she had just told him. Tears of sorrow flow down her cheeks as she feels she has lost both her children to one person – Julian. As a mother, her pain of not being able to help either one of her children is the type of pain she can't fully explain to anyone. She has to rely solely on her faith in God. At this very moment, she has to assure her son that he will be okay and that she is with him spiritually. She yells, "Shawn, Shawn, please pick up the phone and listen to me. Shawn, I love you."

Just as she says those words, Slim picks up the phone. As he hears his mother's voice, a sense of calmness overcomes him and reality sets in. "Mom, did I kill my sister or her baby? I don't understand what happened."

His mother replies, "I love you, Son. Everyone has a choice and Charlene chose that. I will support both of you as my children. I will make sure she is alright. Just take care of yourself."

Through his steady flow of tears he says, "Mom I love you too. I am sorry." Slim hangs up the phone and walks with the guard to the populated area.

"Yo, ain't your little cousin in the County?" Slim says to another inmate.

The inmate responds, "Yeah, Carl just got caught for the drive-by he did about a month ago. He hit like three people. Two of them died, but the one that lived snitched on that dude. Now he about to get some real time. But why you asked me about that dude?"

Slim replies, "Listen, it ain't no beef or nothing like that. I don't know if he wants to make some money since he going to be there for a while, so contact him as soon as possible and let me know what's the verdict." They shake hands and go their separate ways.

Slim lies in his cell bed as he thinks of all the things that have happened in his life. As he visualizes important moments in his life, he goes to the unfortunate incidents in his memory. He tries to figure out where he went wrong. He never thought he would end up in a jail cell for murder. Maybe drugs, but how did it come to murder? He gets angry with himself as he realizes this is the reason he has gotten here. "If I wasn't so angry with Julian, I would have noticed my sister's pain. I haven't prayed in a long time, but God, whoever you are, please don't let my sister or her baby die. My mother needs Charlene's kind heart and loving ways." Slim sits up on the bed in disbelief of his own words and thoughts. His thoughts are interrupted by a knock upon his cell

"I sent the word out and I will get back to you when I hear something, but my dude, what do I get for the connection though?" the inmate asks.

Slim smiles as he says, "I was wondering when you were going to ask me. I can have my chick put something on them books, but furthermore you will have my loyalty."

"Cool, I damn sure can use some dollars on the books, but your loyalty is worth more than a dollar. So we good then, Bro?" the inmate says.

Slim and the inmate give each other a pound in agreement. "Damn, I need to get up and stay in shape. One of these dudes might try me," Slim says as he drops to the floor and starts doing his pushups.

*****

"Meet me at the cell after chow. Plans have changed," Andrew's cellmate says.

Andrew watches him aggressively swallow his food and he nods yes. The way he was approached makes him feel like something is wrong with their agreement.

"Listen, you have about two weeks to get that shipment here. I trust that there is no problem with my request!"

Andrew responds, "No, man. We're good. I will give her a call and see what day she could come up here in the next two weeks. I'll go make that call now." He looks at the time and says, "It's 3:00. She should be just getting home. So after the call I will let you know what day she'll be here."

The cellmate looks at Andrew, slowly nods his head, and says, "Don't disappoint me and we will be the best of friends." He pats Andrew on the shoulder and walks out of the cell toward the population.

Andrew sits on his cell bunk while he thinks of how he can get out of this situation and who could help him. He knows he has no one to help him and he is as good as dead if he doesn't deliver on the request. A sudden thought pops into his head. He says low, but out loud, "I need to speak to my lawyer and tell him everything. Better yet, he can get Detective Jean. She believes me. Yeah, that's what I'm going to do."

Andrew leaves the cell, walks toward the guard, and says," Could you arrange for me to call my lawyer and Detective Jean in Homicide?"

The deputy replies, "Sure, give me a minute and I will find you to make that phone call. A few moments later, the deputy walks up to Andrew and says, "Smith, you can come with me now."

Andrew politely obliges, knowing the reason for the deputy approaching him. The other inmates look strangely at Andrew. They seem confused as to why he would be called to go with the deputy without any reason. His cellmate locks eyes with Andrew and watches him walk with the deputy until he can't see him anymore.

"Hello, Mr. Kepozy. This is Andrew Smith and I need to speak with you about my case, but I need you to do me one favor. Tell Detective Jean I would like for her to be present."

"I can definitely arrange for her to be here, but may I ask why you want her present?" Mr. Kepozy asks.

"I have new information for her case," Andrew replies.

Mr. Kepozy seems confused when he says, "If there is new information, shouldn't we discuss this before you meet with her? Don't you want to know if this statement could be detrimental to your case before you disclose it?"

"At this point, nothing can save me, but if I can save someone else then I will tell it without discretion. Thank you for doing your job, but you can't help someone whose soul is empty. So please follow through with my request for both of you to be present."

"I'll set up a visit soon and I will contact Jean to attend as well," Mr. Kepozy agrees. "Hey, don't give up. You have a chance of getting a lesser sentence."

Andrew is silent as he listens, but he knows those words are not reality for his life. "You have a good day, Kepozy. I hope to see you soon." Andrew hangs up the phone and is escorted back to the floor with the other inmates. He knows he has to come up with something quick before everyone looks at him as a snitch. There are set times to use the phone, so if you are not using the phone during those times, it's said that you could be getting with the deputies and snitching.

He walks up to his cellmate and says, "Man, I contacted my lawyer so he can get my lady up here for the visit, and I wanted to know how my case was going. I haven't heard nothing from this dude since I went to the arraignment. Shit, my trial is coming up real soon and I don't have a clue what his strategy's gonna be."

Andrew waits for the response of others around him so he can be assured it made sense to them. One inmate responds sarcastically, "Shit, if you got a public defender you won't know anything until you are sentenced." He and a few other inmates chuckle.

Andrew laughs with them as he says, "I'm gonna go write this letter to my lady so she knows to come to the visit." He walks away from the crowd toward his cell.

Andrew walks into his cell and looks for his stash so he can get some relief from the stress. "If I'm going to die, I want to die happy and carefree," Andrew says as he opens the package to put on his mirror. He looks around as he positions himself on the floor behind the bunk beds. He sniffs one line. He feels a sudden rush upon his body and smiles. "This that good shit and I don't give a damn about nothing or no one.

Yeah, it's about me and what I want. He lays his head back and falls into a complete daze.

"I know this dude ain't snitch," the cellmate says to himself. "I haven't seen him write a letter to anyone since he been here. I will kill this motherfucker myself if he even think about snitching." He looks around suspiciously to see if any guards are watching him as he heads to his cell. Andrew's actions tell his cellmate something isn't right, but he knows he must be cautious. If Andrew did indeed snitch, they will guard him closely.

*****

"I just got off the phone with my mom and she told me Andrew's in here. Slim needs me to talk to him and tell him to keep his head above water," the inmate says.

Carl replies, "So Slim wants me to talk to his cousin Andrew? I mean, I don't have a problem with having a conversation with anyone, but what will I get for my trouble? I mean, dudes be trying to be tough in here."

"As far as I know, it ain't nothing but love," the inmate says. "For your hard work, he will put some commas on it for your family. All you have to say is you will definitely have that talk with him and the love will be shown from there on."

"Say less, my dude. Conversation has been confirmed," Carl replies.

"So what you're saying is you gonna talk to this dude soon? Because he needs some to hear some real street shit."

"Man, everybody needs to hear the truth," Carl says. "The street don't love nobody. Furthermore, I need to make sure he's safe in here from other dudes that may want to hurt him. So when did he want me to put some knowledge in his heart?"

"You need to talk to him as soon as possible because you know dudes come here and get a change of heart. So when your girl comes, I hope you can tell her about your heart to heart with Andrew and she can give you some advice on how to go about that conversation."

*****

Andrew's cellmate stands in the doorway, looking at Andrew lying against the bunk, seemingly lifeless from afar. He is unsure if he wants to approach him. He may bc dead already. "Damn, how could he be dead already? Who the hell he pissed off besides me?"

His main purpose for coming in the cell is to make sure Andrew is not snitching, so he slowly approaches his body, looking around to make sure that none of the guards or inmates are paying attention. "Yo, Andrew," he says as he is approaching him. There is no response from Andrew. He reaches down to feel Andrew's pulse. It's faint, but he is alive.

As he looks up to make sure no one is watching, he slaps Andrew across the face to awaken him. Andrew's body jerks, but this doesn't help him wake up. The cellmate is feeling frustrated as he raises his hand again to slap him again. This time his eyes open, but he falls back to sleep. The cellmate stands in confusion. He needs to know if Andrew snitched before he dies. He also wants his supplies delivered as he agreed to. He looks around the cell, thinking about how he could wake Andrew up without alarming anyone else. Suddenly, an idea comes to him. He picks Andrew up and puts his head in the cold water in the toilet. Andrew begins to slowly move. He waits a few seconds and puts his head in there again. This time he feels some resistance from Andrew, so he knows he is slowly coming to. He waits a few more seconds before he does it again. Now Andrew is blowing bubbles because he is trying to talk and resist with his greatest strength.

The cellmate lets him up, then throws him against the wall and says, "What you in there telling them deputies? Because you have not written anyone since you been in here."

Through the coughing and grasping for air, Andrew says, "My girl didn't answer the phone so I called my lawyer to tell him I need a visit, and that I need to talk to him about my case. I swear, man. That's all it was."

The cellmate looks at Andrew harshly. "I know one thing. You better have my shit here next week, because I don't mind losing a junkie roommate. Oh, by the way, the stunt you pulled trying to kill yourself before I got to you, it was cute, but I will keep you alive so I can kill you the right way. Look into your eyes while you suffer." He taps Andrew on the shoulder as he walks out of the cell to continue with his day.

"Forget all these motherfuckers. He gonna threaten me like I'm afraid to die. I was dead before I got here and I don't care about nothing except getting my truth out and staying alive long enough to put all you motherfuckers under the radar." Andrew grabs his stash and he begins to sniff some more. He has no way out of any situation he has been caught up in, so he decides to waste the rest of his life not caring, as this temporary fix feels like the best option to soothe his pain.

*****

"Can you believe this motherfucker done sent a hit out on little Andrew? Yo, he used to protect this dude because he kept getting robbed until they found out who his people was. Crazy thing is, that's his blood cousin and this dude talking about paying me with loyalty," the inmate says, chuckling.

The other inmate replies, "I'm not sure who Andrew is, but I do remember when Slim beat the shit out of your little brother. Yes, when you was locked up the last time. I mean teeth and blood everywhere. He didn't have to do little man like that, though."

Carl's cousin responds, "Oh, yeah. I totally forgot he did do that to my little brother, but hey what can you do when the little dude wanted to be grown and run the streets?" They both agreed and changed the subject.

As the other inmate carries on the conversation, Carl's cousin goes into a complete daze. He had forgotten Slim was the reason why his mom sent his little brother to live with their father. He hadn't seen Slim in a while, so his anger for him calmed as time passed on. Sitting there thinking of the whole incident, he recalls the memories of seeing his brother after surgery. He looked like a different person with all the facial injuries. "Loyalty, my ass. Pay me so I can definitely pay you back later." A sudden rage overcomes him as he bangs on the table and says, "This motherfucker ain't loyal to no one, but I know who he will be loyal to."

*****

"35, 36, 37, 38, 39…" Slim trails off when he looks up and sees a shadow over him. He gets up to greet the person who has interrupted his workout. "You need something? I'm just doing my daily exercise."

The deputy responds, "I don't need anything, but you are called for a visit."

Slim gets back down to do his pushups. "I don't know about nobody visiting me. My mom is working and I don't have no friends, so I'm confused." He looks up at the deputy with confusion on his face, trying to figure out who it could be.

"So are you refusing the visit? Because if not, we have to go now."

Slim replies, "I'm not refusing the visit. I'm coming with you now." He gets up and follows the officer to the visiting area. The deputy searches his name in the computer to see which seat he will be assigned to.

As the deputy walks him over to be seated, Slim is looking around to see if he notices anyone he knows, but he doesn't know anyone that's waiting in the visiting area. They come to a stop at the table he will be sitting at and he looks very confused as he slowly sits down. He hesitates to pick up the phone because the last time he got a surprise visit, it was not for anything good. He picks up the phone and asks, "Who are you and why are you here?"

The woman replies, "I put some money on your books and I came to keep my promise of holding you down." Slim is trying to make sense of what she's saying. She notices he looks very confused so she says, "Christine sent me," without making any sound. Slim can't make out what she is trying to say, so she says it two more times until he catches on.

Slim drops the phone and jumps up. "Yo, deputy. I need to go to my cell right now. I'm done with this visit. The guard asks Slim if he is having any problems. He responds, "Just please take me back to my cell."

The deputy does as Slim requested, leaving his visitor there looking puzzled. She came to inform Slim that Christine has kept her end of the bargain. Mission accomplished.

CHAPTER SIX

~ Gaining Control ~

"I found the perfect spot. You should be able to see the bed from here. Matter of fact, let me record now to see if this shit gonna work," Reggie says aloud as he puts the phone in place and turns the camera on. He plays around with the pillow on the bed as if it was Heavenly in the exact position he is going to put her in. "Yeah. Right here. You can see everything from here. Every stroke." Reggie chuckles. He jumps up from the bed to see what he has recorded and how clear the video came out. He picks up the phone to play the video back. "Damn, that video is pretty clear. Good view and I look like a damn porn star. Game time. This bitch about to be in love after tonight." Reggie places the camera back on the dresser and goes into the bathroom with Heavenly.

"Hey, I'm coming in," Reggie says as he knocks on the bathroom door.

Heavenly replies nervously, "Come in. I'm in the shower." She's nervous because Reggie has never really seen her naked, but she knows that this could possibly be it.

"Hey, I got rid of that phone and threw it in the garbage after I destroyed it. So you ready for me to wash your back?" Reggie asks.

Heavenly looks Reggie in his eyes, hesitating to respond. "Yeah, I guess so."

Reggie sees the hesitation and nervousness in Heavenly, so he knows that in order for her to feel comfortable, he has to be very gentle and considerate. He begins to remove his clothing to get in the shower with her.

Heavenly is slightly shaking because she doesn't know what Reggie's next move will be. She wants him to touch her because she wants him, but she has never done this before.

Reggie looks at Heavenly and grabs the rag to lather it so he can wash her back. "Turn around so I can wash your back. Better yet, I'm going to get in with you." Reggie starts to slowly wash Heavenly's back from her neck down to her curvy bottom. He doesn't want to scare her, so he gently washes her back in a small, circular motion. As he washes up and down her back, he can feel goose bumps on her skin. He begins to slightly massage her so she can relax and feel comfortable. "Are you okay? Because if you're not, I will get out of the shower," Reggie says.

Heavenly replies, "I'm not scared, just a little nervous. I've never been naked or this close to any man." She shyly turns around and kisses Reggie on his lips to let him know she is ready for him. He gently kisses her back as he slowly guides her body to the back of the shower wall. He starts gently kissing her breasts while he holds her hands in his hands against the shower wall. Heavenly has no control over what's happening. She just looks down at Reggie as she feels a sudden hot flash.

Reggie continues to manipulate her breasts. He moves from her breasts to her stomach. As he gets down to her waist, he licks and sucks on her hips and curves. He releases her hands to kiss her inner thigh. Heavenly starts to tremble as she feels passion running through her body. She grabs Reggie's head in an attempt to stop him, but he gently puts her hands to the side as he gently lifts her left thigh. Massaging her thigh, he gently places kisses close to her sea of lust. Reggie looks at Heavenly as he places her leg across his shoulder and continues to kiss her inner thigh.

Heavenly's right leg is trembling. She feels weak and confused. Every time Reggie breathes, she can feel a sensation flow through her body. Reggie moves his gentle kisses slowly over to her sea of love as he places his closed mouth directly on her ocean. Heavenly jumps. This feeling is different than the sensation she has been feeling. She can't describe it, but all she can think is, "What is this feeling? What's happening? Why do I feel so weak? I can't…" She looks down at Reggie.

Reggie tightly grips her inner thigh with his right hand, wanting her to feel how he is in control, but won't hurt her. Laying kisses around his hand on her thigh, he makes his way back to her ocean of love as he rests her leg back on his shoulder. Gently, he parts her sea so he can have direct access to her island. "Baby, I just want to make you feel good. Please relax," Reggie says, speaking these words directly to her exposed island.

Heavenly is going crazy mentally. It feels good, but the tingling feeling has her so confused. All these emotions have her responding back in a vibrating tone as she says, "Mmm, okay."

Reggie now knows she has given him permission to finish what he is doing. With her island exposed at face level with Reggie, he gently rubs it and begins to lick it with the larger part of his tongue, so she can feel all the warmth of his mouth.

Heavenly yells out sensually, "Oh, what the…." She can't finish her sentence.

Reggie knows he is doing something she likes, so he continues laying gentle kisses and warm licking as a combination of lust. Heavenly's breathing and moans become louder with every kiss. Her legs tremble uncontrollably. Reggie knows she is almost at her climax, so he wants to take her there right now. "Baby, if you feel too weak, grab me for support."

Heavenly nods her head because she has become so tense she is about to explode. He dives deep into her island and ocean, licking and sucking fiercely until Heavenly busts. "Reggie, I can't, I'm about to fall. I don't know, Reggie…" Heavenly says as her body jerks from the orgasm.

Reggie slowly puts her leg down and holds her body up with his hands. Feeling satisfied with his performance, he tells

Heavenly to slow down her breathing so she can calm down. "Baby, slow down, take slow deep breaths, look at me, and follow my lead." He demonstrates as Heavenly follows his lead and her breath slows down.

Heavenly feels a sudden sensation that makes her body jerk and she starts back breathing heavily as she hysterically says, "What's happening to me? What have you done to me? I can't control my own body."

Reggie talks to her and explains to her that she had an orgasm and that is normal. He notices Heavenly is not calming down, so he needs to act quickly. He holds her close to him thinking she will relax, but she only goes into another emotional state. "Heavenly, baby, look at me. Stop crying. It's normal to feel this way for your first time. I'm sorry, baby. Did I hurt you?" Reggie says as he comforts Heavenly.

"This is so weird. I don't know why I'm still shaking and I feel weak," Heavenly says as she lays her head on Reggie's shoulder.

He holds her tightly until she is comfortable and stops shaking. He then washes her body with soap from head to toe as Heavenly seems to be off in a daze. She rinses the soap off her body and gets out of the shower to dry off before she returns to the bedroom. She doesn't put any clothes on. She gets directly under the covers, for she is now totally vulnerable to Reggie. Heavenly tries to wrap her mind around what just happened with her and Reggie, but she is slowly drifting off.

Meanwhile, Reggie is in the shower washing up as he thinks of his experience with Heavenly and how vulnerable he knows she is right now. He has a small smirk on his face as he realizes he has to finish executing his plan. He is very proud of himself because he knows his mission is to gain control. As he dries his body off, he thinks of parts of his game plan. He has to get this video down and sent to Christine. He prepares himself to step into the room because he can't seem so cocky. He has to seem sincere and understanding.

Walking out of the bathroom, he notices that Heavenly is sound asleep. He goes over to the phone after making sure Heavenly is asleep. The phone has captured all of the activity for the last forty-five minutes, but Reggie knows he has to delete that video, or there won't be enough storage to record what he needs. He deletes the previously recorded video so he can put the new footage on it. He sits the phone back in place on the dresser so he can continue with his original plan.

Reggie walks over to the bed and looks at Heavenly sleeping. She looks so innocent, he doesn't want to bother her peaceful sleep. He knows now is the time to execute his plan to seduce her. He gently slides the blanket off her to admire her beautiful body. She is so comfortable, she doesn't even realize that he is standing over her. As she lies on her back and takes slow, deep breaths, Reggie gazes upon her, knowing he has to finish his mission. He takes a deep breath as he goes forward with his mission and slides into the bed with Heavenly.

He lies next to Heavenly as he looks at the ceiling in deep thought. His thoughts go over all the events from the past couple of months. "How did I get here? I just wanted to make money and make a difference within my family," Reggie whispers to himself. He has a daughter Heavenly's age. As he glances at Heavenly, that thought runs across his mind constantly, but this is business. How can he put his heart into business? If he follows his heart and lets her go, he knows Theresa will still kill him and all his loved ones.

Heavenly has bought him time to come up with a plan, but he realizes he has gotten lost in this new game his is playing with Theresa. "How can I maintain this life with Heavenly, keep Lisa and the kids happy from afar, but most of all, stay alive to execute all this without harming anyone? Lord, I don't know what happened. How do I correct my mistakes?" Reggie says to himself. His eyes become somewhat cloudy. He rubs his eyes as he focuses back on the situation at hand.

He rolls over and stares at Heavenly, knowing this is her last moment of being a little girl. He can't focus on that right now. He has a point to prove and he needs to do what he said he was going to do – send their sex video to Christine. He positions himself in between Heavenly's legs and pushes them apart into a V shape. He softly begins to kiss on her ocean. Heavenly awakens and looks down, seeming confused. Reggie whispers into the opening of her ocean, "Baby, relax. I just want to taste you."

Heavenly tries to relax, but she is nervous again from the experience she had earlier in the shower. As Reggie continues to softly lay kisses on her ocean, he reaches his hand up her body to gently manipulate her nipple. Heavenly speaks in a soft, low moan of lust as she closes her eyes. " Oh…." Reggie reads her body language and hears her cries of pleasure, so he continues to give her more. Sucking softly on her clitoris as he has a conversation, he brings his tongue into his wordplay, licking her in a circular motion. Heavenly is so wet and excited, her legs begin to vibrate from the extreme pleasure. He can feel the waves getting stronger from her ocean, and he continues to work his way to her inner thigh with gentle, manipulating bites as he massages her neck at the same time. Slowly, he goes up her thigh to her hip and then her stomach, manipulating both back and forth as he gently slides his middle finger inside her ocean.

Heavenly's head is rolling from side to side as she loosely says, "What the fuck are you doing to me?"

Heavenly has not yet realized that Reggie has penetrated her with his finger because her mind is going in so many directions. Reggie knows if she has let him slide his finger in without much resistance, he will continue to listen to her love language until the time is right. He continues his manipulation of her body, knowing this is the right time and he is going swimming in the deep end.

He slowly climbs right up to her ocean. Heavenly's eyes are still closed. He looks down at Heavenly and kisses her passionately. She opens her eyes briefly and she begins to kiss him back, feeling the warmth of his stick. He continues to stare at Heavenly as he brings his stick of fire directly to her ocean. Reggie braces himself so he can have total control of his stroke and gently releases the first one. There is no difference in Heavenly's facial expression because he has not yet entered her ocean. It's hard for him not to go full throttle after he feels her warmth, so he thinks of something else to stay focused. He pushes a little deeper. He can feel the resistance and tight grip of her ocean, but he notices her cringe a little from this stroke. He manipulates her breast with his warm tongue, wanting her to stay relaxed. He can feel her loosen slightly, so now he can go deeper, but gently.

"Is this what you want?" Reggie asks.

"Yes, but it hurts a little," Heavenly replies through her deep breaths.

Reggie replies seductively, "I will never hurt you, baby. Just take slow, deep breaths and try to relax. It won't hurt so much."

Heavenly closes her eyes and takes a slow, deep breath. Reggie manages to get all the way in and now he is in control. As he takes slow strokes in and out of her ocean, he is careful not to pull back too far. He pushes his fire stick firmly against her pelvis as he passionately kisses her. Heavenly has short delays between her breaths as she tries to endure the pain.

Suddenly, it goes from pain to pleasure. As Reggie listens to her love language, he knows he is near the right spot. He grabs her round, firm bottom and begins to grind in a circular motion.

"Oh…" Heavenly says as she clenches her nails deep into Reggie's back.

Reggie begins to pick up the pace. He knows she is nearly about to explode. He presses even closer to her pelvis as he delivers his constant strokes. He knows the closer he is to her, the more he can manipulate her clitoris with every stroke. Her ocean is so wet, he can't help but to tell her how good her ocean feels. "Damn, I'm glad I waited. This shit is so good."

Heavenly suddenly begins to release all over Reggie. She pulls him closer to her as her ocean continues to send out a tsunami of waves on his stick of fire. Reggie knows he only has a certain amount of time before he explodes, so now he has to let his stick of fire bust. He grabs both of Heavenly's legs and places them on his shoulders as he begins to take short, but aggressive strokes. Grabbing Heavenly's neck, he begins to stroke faster and more consistently.

Heavenly is confused and looks at Reggie, trying to figure out what happened to him being gentle, but she notices his eyes are closed now. "Wait, that hurts," Heavenly says through each aggressive stroke.

Reggie opens his eyes and he sees her face is cringing. He looks away and continues to deep stroke her ocean. Heavenly tries to remove Reggie's hand from her throat and reposition herself, so maybe it won't hurt so bad. She realizes Reggie has her pinned down and she can't move, so she has to receive every stroke.

He has lost control, so he doesn't pay any attention to her. His only concern is with busting open his stick of fire and completing his mission. He is focused and aggressive. Heavenly can't get through to him. As he grips her throat tighter with every stroke, Heavenly begins to cough, but he doesn't stop. He can feel her ocean drying up, so he needs to hit every wave with each stroke.

"Please stop," Heavenly says softly through her short breaths.

Reggie hears her cry and releases her neck. He grabs her legs and holds them in as he finishes his deep strokes.

"Ouch, that hurts, Reggie," Heavenly says.

He hears her cries, but he is about to bust, so he becomes more aggressive as he pounds on her ocean. "Damn, girl," Reggie says as his body gives a slight shake. He finishes releasing his stick of fire and pulls it out. As he looks down at Heavenly, he realizes she is no longer pleased with his sex. He gets up as he grabs his stick of fire and heads to the bathroom, ignoring every look of fear Heavenly has on her face.

Heavenly feels extremely moist, so she looks down and touches her ocean. She sees a red, familiar fluid. "Why am I flowing and my stomach hurts? It's not that time of the month yet." She yells for Reggie to come to her aid.

Reggie ignores her cry for him. He is confident of his plan now. "Man, this bitch calling me like I give a damn. That's normal shit when you get busted open for the first time. She better be lucky I went light on her ass, but this is just the beginning. That thang going to be deep when I'm done with her."

Heavenly notices Reggie has not come to check on her yet. She doesn't know what to do, so she grabs the sheet and places it between her legs until she doesn't feel any more moisture. She places the pillow under her head as she lies there and silently cries tears of pain.

Reggie cleans himself up and exits the bathroom. Upon entering the room, he sees Heavenly balled up and red fluid dried up on the sheets. He walks over and tells her to go clean herself up. He can't comfort her right now because the video is still going and he needs to show no remorse for her or her family. "Yo, go get in the shower. I will clean this up," Reggie says.

Heavenly rolls over and heads straight to the bathroom. She sits on the toilet as she runs the water and cries with her head in her hands. "Why, Lord, does it seem all men are out to destroy women? First my dad and now Reggie," Heavenly says as she continues to sob and feel unworthy.

Reggie picks up the phone to see if it is still recording. He notices the video ended at some point. He replays the video. Everything has recorded as planned. He searches in the phone for Christine's name and uploads the video via text message. He stops to think about the effect this is going to have, but he presses send.

He calls the front desk of the hotel. "I need some clean sheets to my room. Thank you," Reggie says. He puts on his underwear and sits on the sofa to watch the basketball game.

CHAPTER SEVEN

~ Lost Souls ~

Mrs. Smith walks up to the nurse to introduce herself and check on her daughter. "Hello, I'm here to see Charlene Smith, my daughter."

The charge nurse responds, "Hello, great to meet you. Nancy has been her nurse on this shift since she came to the unit. I will go get Nancy so she can give you an update on your daughter and the baby's health. She will be able to give you any new information from Charlene's doctor."

Mrs. Smith waits at the nurse's station until Nancy approaches her and guides her to the room. "Hello, Mrs. Smith. I'm Nancy. I am very glad meet you. I must assure you that we have been taking great care of your daughter and the baby." Nancy grabs Mrs. Smith's hand as she says, "I would like to inform you before we go into the room, she has a lot of machines and tubes on her so we can monitor her and the baby. Initially, we thought she was early in the pregnancy, but we have now determined she is at twenty-four weeks. Her system is clear of any substance from the overdose, but we are not sure what kind of damage she has endured at this moment. The baby is developing normally at this time and we put the needed nutrition in the tube. Charlene is breathing on her own now, so if she wakes up from the coma, we will not be giving her any other medicine to keep her coma chemically induced. If they both continue to progress at this level, all machines will eventually be taken off and she will be released with aftercare."

Mrs. Smith thanks Nancy for the update on Charlene and the baby's health as she prepares herself to walk into the room. Nancy and Mrs. Smith walk into the room together because Nancy needs to start her rounds.

As Nancy walks all the way into the room and starts her normal routine, Mrs. Smith suddenly stops at the door. She puts her hand over her mouth as tears flow down her face, and she turns to go back in the hallway. "Look at my baby. Lord, have mercy on my child," Mrs. Smith says as she wipes her tears and prepares to go back into the room.

She pulls up a chair next to Charlene's bed and begins to talk to her. "Hey, baby. It's been a while since I saw you. I know you are getting better; the nurse told me so. I see they have been brushing your hair. It's still so pretty," Mrs. Smith says as she strokes Charlene's long, silky hair. "I'm not sure if you know how far along you are, but they say you are twenty-four weeks. I hope it's a beautiful little girl that will look just like her mother. I would love to comb her hair just like I did yours when you were a little girl."

She smiles as she grabs Charlene's hand and gently caresses it. She looks around at all the machines and cries a few more tears for her daughter and grandchild. She can't imagine the pain both of them have endured in the struggle to stay alive. She gently puts Charlene's hand down and begins to rub her stomach. She rubs all the monitors and begins to speak closely to her stomach. "I know you can hear me, but I want you to know we love you dearly. You are strong because you come from a strong family that can't wait to see you. When you come into this world, I know you will make a difference in everyone's life. We will make sure you know God and his power from birth."

Mrs. Smith begins to gently kiss Charlene's stomach as she attempts to stimulate the baby's senses to know her voice. Suddenly, she seems to feel movement from Charlene. She steps back to see if it was real, but there is no visible movement from Charlene. She sits back in the chair and grabs her purse, pulling her Bible out of it. She begins to say a prayer before opening the Bible. "God, I trust you. I don't understand everything about you, but I know you're with me. I know you love me, and I know you will never leave me. Remind me of this every day, Lord. In Jesus' name, Amen."

She opens her Bible and begins to read Hebrews 11 aloud to Charlene. Mrs. Smith finishes reading the chapter of Hebrew and takes a quick glance at the time. "It's getting late, baby, and I'm going to head home, but I will be here every day until you open your eyes and return home," Mrs. Smith says. She grabs her purse, places her Bible in there, and begins to put on her coat.

She slowly exits the room, never looking back as she walks toward the nurse's station, so she doesn't notice that Charlene has awakened.

"I want to leave my cell phone number in case there is any change in her health," Mrs. Smith says as she writes down her number and hands it to the nurse. She gets on the elevator as she proceeds to leave the hospital.

Nancy walks up to the station moments later and receives the information. "I will update this later. I have to go in and start my rounds," Nancy says as she heads toward Charlene's room. She grabs the chart and rushes over to check her pupils. "Hello, honey, I am so excited you are awake. Can you hear me? Nod your head yes or no." Charlene slowly nods her head yes. "I will be back with the doctor shortly," Nancy says.

She rushes down the hall to the nurse's station. "Charlene Smith has opened her eyes. Do you think I can catch her mother?"

Another nurse replies, "You can try to catch her. I will cover you for a few moments."

Nancy says, "Thank you." As she rushes to the elevator, she looks around to see if she can spot Mrs. Smith. Unfortunately, her attempt to reach her with the great news is unsuccessful. Nancy gets back on the elevator and goes to the floor. "Where is the number she left? I want to give her a call. Hello, Mrs. Smith, this is Nancy, Charlene's nurse. I just want you to know she has opened her eyes right after you left the hospital, but you were already gone. So this is just a courtesy call to keep you updated on her health. Please feel free to give us a call back," Nancy says as she leaves the voice message.

*****

As Mrs. Smith gets in her car, a great feeling of joy overcomes her at that moment. "Lord, I know you gonna take care of my baby. Thank you, Jesus," she says. As she picks up her phone, she notices that her it has died and needs to be charged. "When I get home I'm going to charge my phone. That dang thing keep dying. I'm okay with a house phone." She pulls out of the driveway and begins to drive home.

Approaching her home, she notices a young lady knocking at her door. "Who can this be? She doesn't look familiar. You can never tell with all the women Shawn had been out here messing around with. I don't know why any of them would come here. He don't live here," Mrs. Smith says as she pulls into her driveway. As she prepares to exit the car, she notices the young lady standing with an envelope in her hand. "Hello, may I help you, young lady?" Mrs. Smith asks.

The young lady asks if she is Slim/Shawn's mother. "I know Shawn/Slim isn't here, but he told me if anything happened to him, to give you this envelope." She reaches out her hand to give Mrs. Smith the envelope, but she is hesitant to take it. "Ma'am, I don't mean any harm. I just came to go through with my promise," the young lady says.

Mrs. Smith looks at her and takes the package. "Thank you." She unlocks the door as she watches the young lady disappear down the street. As she enters the house, she lays her things down, sits at the table, and opens the envelope. Her eyes widen as she pulls out the contents of the package and says, "Dear God, where did Shawn get all this money?" She begins shaking her head because she knows this money has come from no good. To accept this money would be accepting his lifestyle.

*****

"Hey, the beautiful and elegant Mrs. Theresa. I have tried to contact you numerous times, but I failed each time. So I'm just going to leave you with all the details I have gathered at this moment. The address for Reggie was not correct; that is his child's mother's residence. I also have another address I found in Florida for him and I am going to check things out. My flight leaves at 2:30 and I will arrive around 4:00 pm. I will check into the hotel and then contact you to see if you have received my message, otherwise I will head over to the address

I found and check things out. I will be staying a few days to see what information I can get or if I find Reggie himself. So talk to you soon, and yes I still want my date, lovely lady," Richard says as he chuckles and ends the voicemail. Richard grabs his bag and heads out the door on his way to the airport.

"Welcome to Orlando, Florida," is announced over the PA system. Richard grabs his bag as he exits the plane and turns his phone off airplane mode. He waves down a cab so he can go to the hotel and check in. "Do you know where Hotel Blue is located?" Richard asks the cab driver.

The cab driver replies, "Sure do. It's about eighteen minutes away from here." He pulls out of the airport and heads to the hotel.

"Thank you for getting me here safely, sir," Richard says as he hands the driver the money for his fare. He grabs his bags and proceeds inside the hotel to check in. "Reservations for Mezz, Richard that is," Richard says as he approaches the desk clerk.

She looks up his name, hands him paperwork, and takes his card to charge it for the room. "Here is your key, sir, and is there anything else I can do for you?" the clerk asks.

Richard replies, "No, there isn't. Thank you. Which way do I go to get to my room?"

The clerk replies, "Go around this corner to the left and go down a little ways and you will see the elevator on the right."

"Thank you," Richard replies. He heads to the elevator.

Richard enters the room and starts to put his things away. He realizes he will need a car to travel because it will become very expensive to use a cab, so he calls to reserve a rental car at the nearest place. "I will be there to pick it up in the next thirty minutes," Richard says as he confirms with the rental agency.

"It's still daylight so I have time to investigate this address I found." Richard puts his things away and goes to get the rental.

As he enters the lobby of the rental establishment, he looks around for someone to assist him. A young lady comes up to the desk and says, "How may I help you? I hope you weren't waiting too long. I was in the back checking a car back in."

Richard replies, "You are fine. I was not here very long. So, you have my reservation for Richard Mezz?"

The clerk looks into the computer and finds his reservation. "I have you right here for a midsize." Richard hands her his information and she goes to the copier to print out some paperwork. "So, I'm going to run your card through the system. In the meantime, sign where I have placed the Xs and read in full before signing."

Richard rented a car before, so he does not read the paperwork in full content. He hands her the paperwork and she takes him outside to the car he will be renting. She explains the contract agreement and gives him the car so he can pull off and start his evening.

Richard puts the address he found in the GPS so he can easily get to his destination. He turns on soft, classical music; this is his favorite music to ride to and keep his mind clear. Richard reaches his destination, but the homes on the street have grabbed his attention. "These homes are absolutely beautiful, and look right there – one for sale." He slowly rides through the neighborhood and comes to a stop at his destination. He notices there is a young toddler playing in the yard with what looks like a teenage young lady. He pulls out photos of Reggie and his known family. This young lady appears to be his daughter from the file Richard has created.

He gets out of the car and approaches the children in the yard playing. "Hello, my name is Richard. I am looking into buying the house up the street. Are your parents home so I can speak with them?"

The young lady replies, "Hello. I am Sadie and this my little brother Reginald. My grandmother and stepmom are in the house." She grabs junior and heads in the house to get the adults. The adults come out and introduce themselves as well.

"Hello, I am Irma and this is my daughter-in-law, Lisa. How may we help you, sir?"

At that moment, Richard knows he has the right house, as he had studied the file previous to his visit. Richard replies, "I am new around here and am thinking about purchasing the home down the street. I was leaving the house to make my final decision, but I'm glad there are neighbors out so I can get a personal opinion about the neighborhood. So, how long have you been in this neighborhood, Mrs. Irma and Mrs. Lisa, if you don't mind me asking?"

Irma replies, "I have been here for over twelve years. My son bought this house for me."

Then Lisa replies, "I am here visiting for a while, but this is my fiancé's mom's house."

"That's great to hear, Mrs. Irma. Do you mind me asking, is your son here?" Richard asks.

Lisa quickly jumps in with a reply. "He is on a business trip, but he will be back soon."

"Well it seems like you all are more than happy here," Richard says. "Twelve years is a long time."

Mrs. Irma chuckles. "The best decision my son made was to get me away from that crazy city. I have been at peace ever since and the neighbors are all nice, even the neighborhood leader. It's a little expensive if you ask me, but it keeps us safe from all the things going on elsewhere. Did they tell you we pay $200 dollars a year for the superintendent of the neighborhood? He's okay, but hell, I can use that to delegate some damn rules."

Richard says, "I totally agree with you. That's a lot of money in addition to the taxes they already have set up. Overall, I think it's worth it and the neighborhood is beautiful. I gotta run, but it was nice meeting you both. By the way, Lisa, where are you from, if that isn't too much to ask?"

"New Orleans, and I'm tired of this quiet place. I need to hear some noise!" Lisa replies.

Richard gives a little giggle at her comment as he heads back to the car. He picks up his phone to give Theresa a call.

CHAPTER EIGHT

~ The Awakening ~

"This damn girl done sent this chick I don't know to visit me. This chick is a damn dollar and I'm not free to spend it. Man, this shit is entirely too much. I'm trying to get the fuck out of here. I gotta put a rush on this shit because I see people are getting careless and don't care. Shit, she got kids and her family. All I got is my momma and sister. I definitely ain't letting shit get in the way of me possibly coming home to my family. Is she trying to set me up again? Only person who can connect us two is Andrew, and he about to be done."

Slim jumps up off his bunk and heads to the mess hall. He needs to find his homeboy so he can put a rush on the hit for Andrew. Looking through the crowd, he spots his homeboy and waves for him to come talk to him. Slowly his homeboy approaches and takes a seat with him to see what he is inquiring about.

"Yo, Dee. Man, I need a rush on what I asked you to do for me. I'm gonna hit ole girl tonight. She will be here to visit you as soon as she can and we gonna link to get that done. This bitch done sent some strange chick to visit me."

Dee replies "Yo, what she want, Slim? That's crazy. Ya'll got a case together and she sending people at you. You think she trying to roll over on you, yo?"

"To be honest, I definitely don't trust this bitch. She got something up her sleeve, though," Slim replies.

Dee replies, "For real, she grimy like that, yo. Yeah you better take care of loose ends if you want to see the daylight outside these walls. So with that being said, I'm gonna get on the phone and make that as soon as possible. But yo, on some real shit, what you offering me or what do I get out of this?"

Slim responds, "Yo, really you didn't have to ask. Whatever the fuck you want, you will get as long as it is within reasonable guidelines. I need to get this right. All I can think of is my mom and my sister. Ole girl said she just put bread on my books. I can transfer that over to your account, or I can just give my account info so you can order some commissary. I got shit put up out there, so I'm not worried about this petty cash in here," Slim says.

Dee looks at Slim, slaps him up in agreement, and walks away. Slim sits at the table with his head in his hands, hoping that things go according to plan. This whole case has been so stressful for him and he doesn't want to kill his own blood, but it's either him or Andrew.

"Yo, what's up?" the inmate says.

Slim feels a slight tap on the shoulder, startling him. He looks up to see who is in his presence. "Man, what's up with you?" Slim asks. They slap each other up and start an unwanted conversation.

"They said you was in this motherfucker for killing that church boy…mmm, what's his name?" the inmate says.

"Man, I was sitting here in my thoughts. You know the code. We don't talk about our case, man," Slim replies.

"You right, man. I just was thinking you could have beat his ass and been good with that. I meant, he ain't a reason to do real time. You feel me?" the inmate says with a chuckle.

Without moving his head, Slim glances at the inmate as he says, "I don't want to talk about that shit, man. I'm here to do my time for whatever they say I did. Furthermore, who the fuck are you? The police?" Slim gets up and walks away from the inmate.

The inmate yells as Slim is walking away, "Yo, my bad, Slim. I didn't mean no disrespect, my dude."

Slim throws his hands up as if to say they were cool and it's over now.

*****

"Hey, Auntie. How have you been?" Dee asks.

"I am great, baby. How are you?"

Dee replies, "I'm hanging in there, you know. It's hard, but can't do nothing but take it one day at a time."

His aunt softly replies, "Well, honey, it seems that you handling it the best way you can. God loves you even when you don't love yourself. I love you too."

Dee replies in a sad, but soft voice, "I love you too. Thank you. That made my day. By the way, have you spoken to Carl lately? How is he doing?"

"Yes, he is okay. He's just so young down there in those people's prison. I spoke with him earlier. I reckon he will call back after awhile. Is there something you want me to tell him?"

Dee replies, "I'm glad to hear he's holding up, but I wish he would have made better choices and learned from my mistakes."

The voice on the phone reminds them they have only sixty seconds until the call ends. Dee rushes to get his words out before the call cuts out, "So, Auntie, tell him I said holla at ole boy Andrew as soon as he hang up with you."

Suddenly, the phone hangs up and their call has ended. Dee feels he has accomplished his mission and wants to tell Slim. As he is walking to the floor to talk to Slim, a vague memory of his brother appears. He feels a sudden anger as he plays out the previous conversation amongst the inmates. "This dude really grown as fuck and stomped my little brother out. Man, I really been waiting for the day to see him," Dee says as he is lost in his thoughts. He is so lost in thought as he is walking, he almost runs into another inmate, but he looks up before he runs into him. Walking across the mess hall to Slim's cell seems so long. He stops in his tracks to get his game together before he reaches his destination.

Dee takes a deep breath as he gets closer to Slim's cell. "Yo, Slim," Dee says as he knocks on the cell to get his attention.

Slim looks up as he realizes who is trying to get his attention. "Yo, what's up Dee?" Slim asks.

Dee says, "I just handled that and sent out the word to Carl. I need to know specifically when you sending that paper, man. I can tell you the job is good as done."

Slim replies, "My dude, I can transfer the max they will allow into your account as soon as we done here."

"Say less," Dee replies. He slaps Slim up and proceeds to the lounge area. Slim lays back down with a smile on his face from the news he had just discussed with Dee.

*****

"Hello, Jean. How have you been?" Mr. Kepozy asks.

Jean replies, "Hello, I am fine. Thanks for asking. May I ask who am I speaking with right now?"

"Oh, I apologize. This is Mr. Kepozy, Andrew Smith's lawyer. I am calling because Andrew requested to speak with you and I wanted to know, what's your availability this week?" he asks.

"I knew the voice sounded familiar. Could you hold for a moment while I take a look at my calendar?"

Mr. Kepozy quickly responds, "Sure, take your time."

Jean places the phone down while she looks through her calendar and she notices that she has two spots open. "Hello, I have an open spot today and one tomorrow at 3:00 pm. Which one works for you?"

"Tomorrow at 3:00 pm would work for me as well," he replies. "Thank you for your time and we will meet in the lobby."

Jean responds, "I will definitely be there a few minutes early. This should be an interesting visit." They both hang up the phone. Jean marks the meeting on her calendar, so she remembers to show up. She knows Andrew has some truth to his story, but does he have something now he wants to admit to her?

*****

"Smith, you have a visitor," the deputy says. Andrew looks up at the deputy, confused because he was not aware of anyone visiting.

His cellmate smiles as he thinks this visit should be for his new product. "Have a great visit, buddy," he says to Andrew.

Andrew looks back at his cellmate. He knows why he is so excited, but he knows this could be his last chance to tell his story before something happens to him. Andrew continues to follow the deputy to the visiting room where his lawyer and Detective Jean are waiting for him.

Andrew walks into the room and a sudden nervousness comes over his body. As he tries to take a seat, he has a slight tremble. "Are you okay, Andrew? You do know this conversation is between us," Mr. Kepozy says.

Andrew replies, "I'm good. Just a little tired. Can I have some water or coffee?" The deputy goes to fetch him some water. As Andrew sips his water, he says, "I know you both want to know why I called this meeting, but I need to tell my side of the story before…." He stops speaking before giving away the fact that he knows he's going to die. He'd rather die from self infliction from the drugs than from the hands of his cellmate. "Anyways, ya'll are here because I want to admit my part and things that I wasn't aware of, but put together. I have been thinking more about it. Listen, I will sign any paperwork you need me to so people will know my story."

"Are you in any kind of trouble that we should know about?" Mr. Kepozy asks.

Andrew replies, "Naw, but listen to me carefully as everything I tell you will be important later. Jean, remember when I told you I thought Christine was Angie Martinez? Well, I know for sure she is the same person. When I found the ID, it dawned on me because of the name, but it was Christine's picture. Slim had told me that Angie came to see him, but he knew she knew the deputy at the desk, so she probably didn't put it in the system. So basically, I was set up. Slim was messing around with her, introduced us so when he killed her husband, I would look like the crazy, jealous lover. I knew he wanted to kill Julian, but not in front of everybody. He had me thinking, I'm fucking this bitch to keep her mouth closed and all along they had a deal to murder Julian."

"Wait, this story sounds familiar. You said all of this when I interviewed you. How will I know you are telling the truth? I never found any identification in the house. If you weren't informed, Christine is out on bail and she got insurance money. They couldn't hold it because we do not have any evidence that she hired him, but she was found to be guilty by association. That association was you and Christine's relationship."

Andrew stares at Jean in disbelief. How did they release the money without a thorough investigation?

Mr. Kepozy jumps into the conversation when he notices the look on Andrew's face. "You can end this conversation whenever you are ready. You seem very uncomfortable right now."

Andrew responds, "I don't understand how ya'll didn't figure this shit out yet." He becomes very frustrated as he slightly raises his voice and says, "There is video footage of the inside and outside of the house. Ya'll dumbass cops never looked at the tape. Me and Slim had a conversation on the couch. We talked about him taking care of Julian and me keeping Christine under control. I…"

Andrew was interrupted by Jean. "Wait, you mean there was footage of the house? I never saw the footage. I need to find that footage." Jean jumps up from the table and excuses herself to make a phone call. "Hey, I was just with Andrew

Smith and he says there was footage inside the house. I'm on my way back to the station," Jean says. She hangs up the phone and enters the room again. She takes a seat next to Mr. Kepozy to finish listening to Andrew's story.

"Kepozy, did you get everything I said as well? Because I need this on record," Andrew says.

"Yes, I did record everything, but I am a little puzzled. Why are you so adamant about telling me this? Are you in trouble or is someone threatening you?" he asks.

Andrew looks at Mr. Kepozy with a consistent, but fearless stare as he says, "If something happens to me, my cellmate did it!" Andrew waves for the deputy to come in and take him back to his cell.

Mr. Kepozy is at a total loss for words and just stares at Andrew. "You know if you don't feel safe, I can pull a couple of strings to keep you safe," Jean says.

Andrew replies, "It's not a matter of me being safe. We are not safe anywhere, no matter how we live. Just know I told my story and you were here to witness it personally."

Jean looks at Andrew, feeling helpless that she is unable to give him any assistance because she doesn't really know what is going on.

Andrew returns to the population and he heads to his cell. His cellmate notices he is in a rush to get through the crowd and that he is trying to go unnoticed. He gets up and follows him to the cell, curious to find out why Andrew is in such a rush. Could he be in a rush because he has the shipment, or has something gone totally wrong?

Andrew approaches the cell in a very frustrated, but blissful manner. He looks for his stash, wanting to forget that he just snitched. The feeling of telling it all made him feel deceitful, but he knows he will die, either from his cellmate's hands, or from his habits.

"My man," says his cellmate, startling Andrew.

Andrew turns around as he's reaching for his stash. "Hey, man. She had me out there waiting, but she didn't show up. They had me in the holding area until visits were done."

His cellmate looks at him, disappointed. "So what you are saying is she never showed up, so there is no supply?"

Andrew replies, "No, she didn't show up, but I'm sure she will be here this week."

The cellmate looks at him with a sinister smile on his face. "So I'm supposed to wait until she decides to come to visit for you to repay me?"

"She usually keeps her word. Something must have happened."

"Right. Well, I guess since you can't keep your word, something must happen to you too. I will definitely deal with you later. I gotta tell the boss the great news." He walks out of the cell as he gives Andrew a look of disgust. Andrew doesn't even let his words sink in before he starts getting high and forgetting about everything.

*****

"Time for breakfast. Wake up, wake up you little girls," says the deputy.

It is time for breakfast and Andrew opens his eyes as if he is surprised he is still alive. Did his cellmate actually believe him and let him live, or is he dreaming? He looks down at his cellmate's bunk and he too is just awakening. Even though he is still alive, he has the fear of not living through tomorrow. "What do I do? Play like I'm still asleep, or do I walk around like nothing is going to happen? Well, it doesn't matter either way. I can't stay in this cell all day," Andrew says to himself.

As he looks out of one eye, playing like he is asleep, he watches his cellmate get ready for breakfast. The cellmate is also looking to see if Andrew is awake. He's not sure of when he will take him out, now or later. He sees Andrew is asleep, so he doesn't bother him. There is no fun in killing a helpless person in their sleep, so he goes off to breakfast like many other inmates.

The guard comes back to the cell to awaken any inmates not accounted for at the mess hall. "Yo, Smith, you need to get to breakfast; you know there's a routine," the deputy says. He walks away, giving Andrew a chance to get up and get ready.

As the deputy walks to the mess hall, he questions an inmate coming toward him. "Where are you going?"

The inmate replies, "I'm going to my cell to get my thermo. I am a little cold, sir."

The deputy says, "Okay. You have a few seconds before we have the count again."

The inmate nods his head in agreement and walks extremely fast. He continuously looks back to see if the deputy is watching him. The coast is clear so he goes into the cell and says, "Hey, what's up Andrew? How have you been? Never mind, it's apparent you're not doing too well. You look like shit, but it doesn't matter because this is about to be messy."

Andrew turns around to face the cellmate. "Who sent you? I can pay more than they are already paying you."

The inmate replies, "Who sent me? You did. The shit you did was obviously fucked up. Your own people want you dead. I just came to do my job, so let it happen and don't make it worse than it has to be."

Andrew looks at him, surprised because he was sure his cellmate sent him, but he's puzzled by the inmate's statement. "Before you do your job, you said my people. Who are you talking about, dude?" Andrew patiently awaits his answer so he can try to understand who in the hell this man could be.

"Yo, Slim sent me to take care of you, so you won't be snitching and make his case harder to beat."

Andrew drops a tear as he looks Carl directly in his eyes. He turns around and falls to his knees, bows his head, and closes his eyes. He begs for forgiveness from God as he knows this is the end.

With no emotion and no remorse, Carl walks up to Andrew and strikes him rapidly in his upper back. Andrew drops to the floor. He doesn't make a sound during his death. Carl watches as his last breaths have been taken.

Carl runs out of the cell to clean himself up. He has extra clothes for the occasion. He quickly throws the clothes in the garbage along with the homemade shank. Carl runs down to the mess hall, slowing down as he gets closer, and then takes a seat.

"Where yo sleepy ass been, dude? I thought you weren't coming," an inmate says.

Carl replies, "Naw, I been down here. I was chatting with a few of my homies, but I'm not that hungry anyways."

"Everyone to their cells now," the deputy says.

"What's going on, Deputy?" an inmate asks.

The deputy quickly responds, "We found one of the inmates assaulted and he is not breathing. So you know we gotta lock it down until further notice."

The whole penitentiary is escorted to their cells until there can be a thorough investigation.

CHAPTER NINE

~ Karma ~

Heavenly turns on the shower slowly as the image of her first encounter flows through her mind. Her movements are slow. She can feel pain with every step that she takes, but her eyes are wide, dull, and still. She sits upon the toilet as she begins to silently weep. "I never imagined my first time being this way. Is this what sex is really all about, or am I just overreacting because I don't know?"

Tears continue to flow down her red, rosy cheeks as she begins to have that feeling again. The feeling of nervousness, being overwhelmed, and distanced from the cold world. The heavier she breathes, the less she feels that this is normal. She doesn't know what's happening, but she has had this feeling in the past. Heavenly drops to the floor to try to maintain her strength because she feels lightheaded as well.

Heavenly cries out to the Lord, "Please stop this feeling. Oh my God, I feel like I am going to die. You said that you will heal any wound. Fix it. Fix it, please."

The feeling lasts for about thirty seconds. Heavenly opens her eyes and she realizes she is on the bathroom floor. She attempts to get up, but her arms are weak and trembling. She seems to be a little confused as she stares at her hand shaking uncontrollably. Just as she is pulling herself up to be able to stand, the door busts open.

"Are you alright? That water has been running…" Reggie says. He stops in the middle of his sentence once he notices Heavenly on the floor reaching to stand. As he walks over to help her, a great sadness fills his eyes. He holds her close as she stiffly lies upon his chest. He gently moves her hair off her face and says, "If by any chance I am the reason you are feeling this way, I'm sorry. I never meant to hurt you. I just became overexcited because your pussy is so good and I haven't had sex in a while. I promise to be gentle if you are comfortable with it happening again."

Heavenly is just standing there, adrift in her own world. Every time she hears him breathe, it reminds her of his breathing pattern during their sexual encounter.

Reggie's heavy breathing is from him being nervous about the way he found Heavenly in the bathroom. Will she try to harm herself, tell the police she was raped, or ruin the plan and call Theresa? Either way, he has to make a fast decision to make her comfortable again. "Go ahead and take a shower. We are still going to dinner if you want to," Reggie says in a very kind voice.

"I think I want room service. I'm really tired," Heavenly says.

Reggie replies, "Well, that would be good too. I will wait until you're out of the shower to order." He knows this type of silence from a female all too well. It's disappointment and hurt in this kind of love language. He walks out of the bathroom and gently closes the door to give her privacy and some alone time.

"Damn…" Reggie says as he walks into the bedroom. "I done fucked up. I don't know what this bitch gonna do, but I know I gotta fix this shit now. I can relax because I already sent the video." He smirks as he feels good to have one up on Theresa, but then he suddenly realizes he has not gotten rid of the phone. He puts on some clothes and prepares to get rid of the phone.

"Hey, I'm going to the lobby to get some menus. I will be right back," he yells to Heavenly from the room. He waits for a response, but she never does respond to him. He grabs the phone and the menu out of the drawer, and then exits the room.

As he enters the lobby, he glances across the waiting area and sees the clerk talking to a Sheriff. He continues to nervously walk toward them as he and the clerk make eye contact while she is still talking.

"I wonder what's going on? I hope no one heard us in the room. Naw, shit, they would have been up there to see what's going on. I'm just going over here to see what the fuck happened. Shit, worst case scenario, they're looking for me and here I am."

Reggie walks over to the two having a conversation and awaits his turn to interrupt. "Are you okay?" he says to the clerk.

She instantly smiles. "Yes, I'm okay. Thanks for asking. How may I help you?"

Reggie knows at that moment they are not there for him or Heavenly. "Could you tell me where the smoking area is?" Reggie asks.

The clerk responds, "Sure. Go out those doors and to the left. I see you have menus in your hand. Do you have any questions I could possibly answer?"

Reggie replies, "Oh these…I totally forgot I had them. What time does the kitchen close?"

"9:00 pm on weekdays, 11:00 pm on weekends. I hope that answers your question."

"Yes, it does. Thank you," Reggie replies.

The Sheriff just stands there and waits for their conversation to end. Reggie walks away and heads toward the smoking area. Once he's outside, he looks around for a garbage can or dumpster. He sees one and begins to walk toward it as he makes sure the phone is off. He throws it in the garbage can and returns to the hotel.

As he enters the lobby to go back to the room, he realizes the Sheriff is still there. He sits near them on a nearby sofa in an attempt to listen to the conversation. "What was the number to the room again? Suite 312?" the Sheriff asks. Reggie becomes more curious once he hears the word 'suite' and they have his direct attention.

"Not suite. Suites are rooms on their own, but Room 512," the clerk assures the Sherriff. The Sheriff walks through the lobby toward the elevators and the clerk goes back to the desk. Reggie is relieved now that he has heard the most important part of the conversation, the room number. He sits for a few more minutes, pretending to watch the TV.

Reggie enters the room and he notices Heavenly isn't out of the bathroom and the bed has been made. Did the maid come and make it? "Heavenly," Reggie yells as he walks toward the bathroom.

Heavenly becomes startled, but replies, "I'm still in the shower. Are you back? Just order me a burger and french fries."

Reggie replies through the door, "I didn't think you heard me, but yeah, I'm back and I will order right now." Reggie places the order as he waits for Heavenly to enter the room.

Heavenly gets out of the shower, dries off, and gets fully dressed. She stops at the sink and looks in the mirror. All she can see is a girl who isn't ready for the real world. "Get your shit ready for the real world. Get your shit together, girl, you're grown now. That ain't shit to cry about. It could be worse. This will all be over soon. Find a job, graduate from school, get new friends, and never tell anyone about who I really am or where I came from." As she lotions her face, she takes a deep breath and walks into the room.

She's fully dressed when she walks into the room, but when she reaches the side of the bed, she wants to be comfortable so she undresses into her panties and bra. Reggie glances at Heavenly as she undresses and he instantly becomes turned on, but controls his urge of wanting to please her. Heavenly notices him watching her as she undresses so she gets under the covers and pulls it up to her neck, still shy and ashamed of the previous events. She lies there as she pretends to watch TV with Reggie.

"How long before the food arrives?" Heavenly asks.

"They said forty-five minutes to an hour."

"I may not eat tonight because I am very sleepy. I really want to get up and go sign up for school. Do you think that will be possible?"

Reggie replies, "Yeah, baby. We gotta get up early anyways. I gotta meet with Johnathan so we can get our new house."

"Okay, I will be up and ready to go," Heavenly says. Meanwhile, she wants to go to sleep, but her mind won't relax from what she just experienced. She also knows that she has to sleep in the bed with Reggie and is not totally comfortable with him.

Reggie looks at Heavenly lying there with the covers over her. They just had sex, so he has seen her whole body. He thinks he knows what he needs to do make the second experience better than the first one. He climbs under the covers with only boxers on and slides closer to Heavenly. He wraps her in the spooning position. His manhood aligns with her womanhood and he begins to grow in length and size. Heavenly becomes nervous instantly and stiffens in one position. Reggie feels her cringe away, so he starts to relax her by rubbing his hands gently across her body.

Heavenly doesn't resist. Even though she would like for him to stop, something in her body is triggered and focused more on his movement across her body. Reggie gently rubs her nipples as he presses his manhood against the opening of her womanhood. He rubs her midsection as he makes his way down to her opening. He notices the more he strokes, the more her natural moisture increases. Once he feels her moisture, he knows this is the perfect time to redeem himself. Heavenly badly wants to turn her emotions off, but she has no control. Now she is craving him, forgetting her experience from the first time.

He slides her panties off and she shows very little resistance, and he removes his boxers as well. He gently pulls Heavenly to her back as he takes control. He notices her eyes show some fear, so he takes that into consideration as he continues to seduce her. He places small, gentle kisses on her lips until she responds and returns the kisses, as his manhood soaks up the juices of her womanhood. He begins to breathe a little heavily, as he knows he must get to it because he only has a few minutes to please her. He opens her legs wide and he wastes no time to please her womanhood. He sucks on her womanhood as he gently slides his finger in the crevices of her womanhood.

Heavenly arches her back as she gives off a small moan. "Oh..." She is so submissive. All her body wants is more pleasure.

Reggie reads her body language and exits her womanhood, so he can expose her mountain top. She doesn't know why she is doing this, but she feels free and relaxed. He continues to read her body language, so he slides his arms under her smooth chocolate bottom as he wraps them around her inner thighs, in an attempt to help her mountain to stay exposed. He sucks, licks, and nibbles on her womanhood from the top of her mountain, until he can taste her cream.

Heavenly arches her back, pushing her womanhood closer and grabs his head so he can lick all the icing off her cake. "Don't stop, baby. Oh my goodness, what the...." Heavenly says faintly.

He gets up and juice is on his face. Passionately grabbing her bottom lip, he slides into her womanhood. "Damn," says Reggie, sounding tired. He braces himself over Heavenly so he can control his stroke as he slowly strokes her ego and pussy. He knows if he is gentle and makes love to her she will look at him differently. He looks in her eyes as he slowly strokes in and out to let her feel and see his compassion for her. Heavenly looks back at him and quickly turns her head and focuses on the feeling, so she doesn't focus on how he violated her.

Reggie notices she has her eyes closed, so he wants her to keep focused as he sucks on her breast and watches her body language. She begins to roll her head slowly against the pillow and he feels that she is relaxing. Slowly stroking her and kissing her body, he feels her legs grabbing tightly to the small of his back. He continues to plant soft, warm kisses upon her body as he slowly grinds his body against her to find her spot. Slowly, Heavenly's mouth comes open with many sounds of pleasure. Reggie knows he must be on the right spot, as he consistently watches her body language.

"Oh shit. I'm about to cum," Reggie says as he presses closer to her mountain and grinds faster in that same spot. Heavenly wraps her legs more tightly around Reggie, holding him in that spot. Heavenly begins to shake and so does Reggie as they explode together. Reggie drops on top of Heavenly, totally exhausted and out of breath as she continues to throb upon his manhood. Both lie there exhausted and amazed at the magic that has happened.

They both close their eyes until they hear a sudden knock at the door. "Your order is here," the room servant says.

Reggie pushes up off of Heavenly, looking into her eyes as he slides out of her womanhood. Heavenly doesn't even notice him staring until he pulls out of her and she feels all of the moisture run down her leg. As she tries to control her breathing and shaking, she takes a few deep breaths in and out.

"Here I come," Reggie says as he rushes to put on some clothing.

"I will leave it right in front of the door, or I can wait if it's not going to be long," the room servant says.

Reggie replies, "I am getting dressed, but I am coming right now." He opens the door, apologizes for the inconvenience, and takes the food.

Heavenly gets up to clean herself up in the bathroom. "I'm so confused. How can you have a bad experience and then enjoy sex from this person? Either way, this sex thing is totally crazy." Confused about her emotions, she washes up and returns to the room. Reggie leaves the room and goes into the bathroom after her. Heavenly begins to eat her food and watch TV.

Reggie looks in the mirror as he says out loud, "What has happened to my life? I was getting money and having fun, but now every inch of my life is a lie." He shakes his head, washes up, and exits the bathroom. "How is the food?" Reggie asks Heavenly.

"It's pretty good. Thank you." She feels a sense of compassion for Reggie. Maybe he didn't want to hurt her.

"Good, because the hotel food can be trash sometimes, so I was just checking," Reggie says. They both chuckle and watch TV until their dinner is finished. "I don't know how long you are going to stay up, but I advise you to go to bed. We got stuff to do in the morning," Reggie says as he gets in the bed and lies down.

Heavenly replies as she is putting her unfinished food on the tray, "Yes we do. I definitely need to go to the school tomorrow." She slowly gets up and holds on to the chair as she feels a throbbing pain between her legs. She slowly climbs into the bed and pulls the covers up on her.

Reggie feels her get in the bed. He rolls over and holds her closely. Heavenly modestly accepts his affection. She hasn't felt this good since her father used to tuck her in and her mother would stand in the doorway and look at her.

*****

"You ready, baby?" Reggie says to Heavenly.

"Yes, baby. I'm ready." Heavenly walks out of the bathroom like a model on the runway. Reggie stops what he is doing and immediately looks at Heavenly. To his surprise, standing there is a Goddess. Hair long and black, not a strand out of place. Smooth, creamy chocolate face matching her beautiful, brown eyes. What is more intriguing is her body, slim and thick. He has to collect his thoughts as he says, "You look good as hell, but let's go. You women take forever."

Heavenly has already caught him staring at her and at that moment, she knows she has his attention.

"Call me when you are ready. I'm going to Johnathan's office to drop this money on the house," Reggie says.

Heavenly replies, "Okay. Remember I don't have a phone." She turns to Reggie and softly kisses him goodbye before entering the building.

CHAPTER TEN

~ No Love Lost ~

"Hello, may I speak with Detective Jean?" Nancy asks.

"This is Jean, but I am not familiar with the name Nancy. How may I help you?"

"I apologize. I am Nancy, a nurse at the hospital. It was noted in my patient's chart, if there was any change in her condition to give you a call. My patient's name is Charlene Smith."

There is an awkward silence between them. "I'm sorry, Nancy. It's a coincidence. I was just working on this case, so it is a surprise that you are calling me. I hope there is good news to be heard."

Nancy smiles as she replies, "I am grateful to be the bearer of good news. Charlene has awakened and is functioning on her own and the baby is doing well also. That doesn't mean there might not still be complications, but it is a good sign. We will run some tests and if all comes back well, she will be released under strict care."

Jean's face brightens up instantly, not because of the case moving forward, but because she has an emotional attachment to this case. "Thank you for the update. If she is to be released, please give me a call with her discharge information," Jean says.

They both agree and hang up the phone. Nancy finishes her notes in Charlene's chart and then pages the doctor again to meet him in Charlene's room.

"Charlene, I have to take your vitals," Nancy says with a smile on her face. Charlene looks at Nancy with her weak, beady eyes, as she nods her head to acknowledge Nancy's presence. Nancy begins to take her vitals which are closer to being normal, when the doctor walks in.

"Hey, Nancy. I see our patient is awake. What other news do you have for me?" the doctor says.

Nancy replies, "Her vitals are better and she is a little more content each time I have come in here."

"Thanks for that report. We're going to run some tests on her and the baby. If all is well, in a couple of days they can be released," the doctor says as he hands the nurse the chart. "Can you get me an emergency sonogram? I want to check the baby's development. Charlene, how are you feeling right now? If you are too weak to speak, you can just nod yes or no to any questions."

Charlene is almost in a state of panic, but she is too weak to display much emotion. "Baby," she whispers softly. She is confused because she doesn't remember being pregnant. She looks down at her stomach as tears roll down her face in disappointment.

The doctor notices she is trying to say something, but is not sure what it is. He comes closer until he can hear her soft words more clearly. "Your baby will be fine. We will give you and the baby all the care that we can give. Someone will be in here shortly to check the baby's health. I see you are tired, so try to relax for your baby's sake. Charlene, you have to calm down…." The doctor is interrupted by the sonographer as she enters the room. "See, they are going to check your baby and you need to really relax." The doctor reassures Charlene that things are going to be okay.

Charlene nods yes to let them know she understands what is going on. Her tears begin to dry up midstream, as she becomes nervous about her baby's health.

The sonographer checks her wristband and begins to set up for the sonogram. "I'm going to take pictures of your baby and also listen to the heartbeat," the sonographer says. Charlene's tears slowly roll down her face as she nods her head yes. Charlene watches the sonographer as she prepares the machine to take pictures. She squeezes warm gel on Charlene's abdomen and places the machine on her to hear the baby's heartbeat. She describes every move she makes to Charlene before she proceeds with the exam. As she finds the perfect spot to place the instrument, she suddenly hears a couple of loud thumps that are steady and rapid. She smiles as she stays steady to hear the heartbeat.

Meanwhile, Charlene begins to cry profusely. Charlene has never heard a baby's heartbeat because her other baby didn't survive. She feels overwhelmed with joy and sadness all at once. All her emotions are showing through her uncontrolled tears.

The sonographer realizes Charlene's emotions are at an all time high. She assures Charlene that the rhythm of the baby's heart is normal. "Does that hurt you, honey?" Charlene nods her head no. "Well, let me tell you, this is a strong, healthy baby. The heart is normal and regular. As I am looking at the size of the heart, that's normal as well." She holds Charlene's hand to help soothe some of her anxiety. "I'm going to take some pictures now. Maybe we can see what the sex will be."

Charlene looks through her blurred vision at the sonographer, who is unaware that this is a bittersweet moment. Charlene thought she was going to wake up in heaven with Julian and her first child, only to realize that she and her second child are still living in this cold world without Julian.

"So, you see this is the top of the head, and I will be measuring the important parts of the baby's body."

Charlene instantly stops crying to focus on the screen.

"So, as you see, your baby is growing on the right track and everything looks good. Wait, hold on…" The sonographer stops her conversation and focuses more intently on the screen.

Charlene becomes wide-eyed as she feels she should be worried. Maybe something is wrong.

"Oh my, this baby is a little stinker. He wants the world to know who he is already."

Charlene has a very confused look on her face. The sonographer just gave her baby a gender – he.

"I am so sorry, look right here," she says as she points to the screen. "That is definitely male parts right there. I see he is not she," the sonographer says as she chuckles. Charlene falls into a long daze, as she is trying to process the bittersweet news.

*****

Mrs. Smith grabs her usual cup of coffee before she goes to work. She sits at the table with her breakfast and coffee as she falls deep into thought. "What did I do wrong with these children? Harold, I wish you were alive. Charlene is in the hospital, pregnant with a child. Shawn is in jail for the murder of the baby's father." She shakes her head in a shameful way as she continues her conversation aloud. "I did what I could. I never thought it would end with both my babies gone. I knew life was gonna bite that boy in the behind, but Charlene – her life was going so good until she met that damn boy. After she met him, I couldn't do nothing with her. She thought he loved her, but he had that other gal. I pray every day, but God knows what he wants for His children."

She places her cup down as she becomes more upset at the thought of her family's current reality. As she sits there stuck in the moment, she suddenly thinks about her phone. She slides from the table and goes to get it. When she comes to the cabinet, she stops because she remembers the money that was in the drawer beneath the phone. She opens the drawer and looks at the envelope, but quickly closes it and grabs the phone instead.

She sits back at the table and turns on the cell phone. While waiting for the cell to turn on, she is easily distracted by the ring of her house phone. "Who could this be this early in the morning? It better be important, interrupting my breakfast," she says as she goes to answer it.

"Hello," she says.

There is utter silence before the person speaks. "Sallie, my boy gone. He gone," says the person on the other end of the phone.

"Edward, this you? What are you talking about?"

Edward replies, "Sallie, listen to me. My boy gone. Them cops called me and said he was into a fight and somebody stabbed him a lot of times. I'm on my way to the hospital to see him now. Lord knows I hope it ain't Andrew," Edward explains to his sister through his grief and tears.

Sallie holds the phone in her hand, at a loss for words to soothe her brother. "I'm going to come with you. Wait for me. I will be right over." She has forgotten what she was going to do as she grabs her keys, cell phone, and purse and then heads out the door.

She pulls up to Edward's house and blows the horn. She is not thinking about how serious and true this really is. "Where is Edward? Got me sitting out here waiting on him," Sallie says as she looks around for him to come outside. She hears her cell phone ring so she is no longer focused on him coming out of the house.

"Hello," she says as she answers the phone. There is a silence and then an automated voice.

"You have a call from inmate "Shawn," he announces himself through the call.

She accepts the call and she tells him all that is going on. "Hello, Son. I hope you are okay in there. I went to the hospital. Charlene and the baby are doing good. She is off the breathing machine and breathing on her own. I'm going back up there tomorrow to check on them."

Slim replies, "Mom, I'm holding on for now. I been working on my mental – reading and writing. I gotta speak to my lawyer this week. I think it might turn out in my favor. I am so glad to hear that she is doing good. So will she be coming home soon, or what they saying?"

Mrs. Smith replies, "I am hoping that she will wake up and come home soon, and have a healthy baby. God is amazing, so she will be just fine." She pauses and takes a deep breath before she says, "On the other hand, your cousin Andrew is not doing so well. They say he died in a fight, but me and Edward are going to make sure they got the right person. Ya'll got to do something different. This family has fallen apart and is now being destroyed."

Slim pauses before he replies. This is good news, but he hates to hear his mother speak this way. He also knows his chance of beating this case just became more of a reality.

"Mom, what happened? Andrew don't mess with no one. How could they have done this to him?" Slim says.

Mrs. Smith says through her tears, "Son, please be careful. My heart can't take all this mess. Here comes Edward, so call me later and I will let you know what happened. Son, pray for the restoration of this family."

"You have sixty seconds left on this call," the automated operator says.

"I love you, Mom. I will call you later. I will pray for our family."

*****

The phone hangs up and Slim walks to the courtyard to look for Dee. He finds him lifting weights. "Yo, it's done. I just talked to my people and they going to view the body. I will send ole girl to Carl and put something on your books as soon as possible. Thanks, man. I see your word is good. I'm in debt to you for life," Slim says. He slaps Dee up and walks away with a sinister grin on his face.

His plan is working out well and now it's Christine's word against his word, despite the confession. Now he can let them know Christine hired him from the beginning.

"Yo, I need to call my lawyer so I can talk to him," Slim says to the deputy.

*****

Sallie lets Edward get in the car and then she pulls off. "I'm sorry, brother. Andrew didn't deserve to die this way," Sallie says.

Edward responds, "My boy ain't no angel out here, but he never been into too much trouble. He got with that boy of yours and it's been trouble ever since." He begins to cry profusely because he knows his relationship with his son was not good.

"You are right and I'm sorry that Shawn got him in all this mess. If Harold was here, he would have been able to guide him better. Ever since his father died he has been different." Sallie looks at her brother with sorrow and compassion.

They enter the parking garage and go into the hospital. As they enter the building, she hears a noise coming from her purse, so she looks for the source of the sound. "Edward, you go ahead. I will be there. Sounds like my phone went off. Where we gotta go anyways?"

Edward replies, "Hell, I don't know nothing about these places. I'm going to go over there and ask that lady at the desk." He walks away and Sallie goes outside the hospital to check her phone.

She removes the phone from her purse and notices she has a few voicemails. She hopes that one of the messages could be some good news. She has had more than her fair share of bad news lately. The first voicemail says, "Sallie, call me. The jailhouse called me and said they taking Andrew to the hospital. I need someone to go with me. Call me back now." She becomes sad from the urgency in her brother's voice. Deleting the message, she hesitates to hear the next one, but she goes forth with it.

The second voicemail says, "You have a call from inmate Shawn." She instantly deletes that message to get to the last one.

The third voicemail says, "Hello, Mrs. Smith. This is Nancy, Charlene's nurse." She takes a deep swallow as she feels this could be good news. She continues to listen closely as the message continues. "I just want you to know she opened her eyes right after you left."

She doesn't finish listening to the rest of the message. Tears flow down her face as she drops the phone and falls to her knees right in front of the hospital, repeatedly saying, "Thank you, Jesus."

She's down on her knees praising God for his work for at least fifteen minutes before anyone notices her. "Ma'am, are you okay? Do you need any assistance?"

Mrs. Smith never even notices the man standing over her until he repeats the same question numerous times. Many onlookers are gathered around to see what is going on. "Yes, sir. I am okay. Praise God," Mrs. Smith says as the security guard helps her to her feet and escorts her inside.

CHAPTER ELEVEN

~ Redemption ~

There's a sudden knock at the door which startles everyone. Theresa walks toward the door and she recognizes the person standing outside. "Take this glass in the kitchen," Theresa says to Lindsey. She was sipping on her everyday drink, cognac. "Christine, you can go let her in. I'm going upstairs to freshen up a bit," Theresa says.

As she goes to answer the door, Christine sprays some air freshener to cover the smell of alcohol that is seeping from Theresa's skin.

"Hello, we have been waiting on your arrival. Lindsey and Mark just came home from school. They are in the family room watching TV," Christine says.

Bonnie greets Christine as well and looks around the house as she enters the family room. "It smells amazing in here. Were you cleaning?" Bonnie asks.

"We were cleaning awhile before you came, but we do clean on a daily basis," Theresa says.

Bonnie looks up at Theresa as she responds to the question intended for Christine. "I meant no harm. Your home is beautiful and clean each time I come here, so I sincerely apologize if I offended you," Bonnie says.

Theresa replies, "No offense taken, love." They all go into the kitchen to discuss the reason for the visit.

"So, you do know why I am here. If not, let me explain my reason for this visit. I would like to finish my paperwork and make a decision, so we either close the case or continue our service. I have to see all the children and speak with them to see if they are taken care of properly. I've seen Lindsey and Mark, but where is Heavenly?" Bonnie asks.

Christine looks as if she is at a loss for words, so Theresa jumps in to answer the question. "Well, we all do know she is now eighteen years old, which means she is considered an adult. She left for school and hasn't returned. Being rebellious if you ask me, but we did speak with her since she left. So we do know she's fine, but just going through one of those teenage stages."

Bonnie writes down all that Theresa has said before she asks, "Did anyone call the police and make a report? I mean, this isn't her normal behavior. She may be in danger somewhere and can't express that over the phone." She looks at both of them, waiting for a response.

Theresa responds, "I figure by now that if we talked to her recently, she is not missing or will be considered missing. Are we concerned? Yes, but she has been through a lot lately. I feel like she is just acting on impulse and don't know how to deal with her emotions."

Bonnie pays close attention to Theresa's response, but she is curious as to why Theresa is doing all the talking. Christine is quiet and this is her child. "Thank you for your response, Theresa, but Christine is her mother. How do you feel about her disappearing?"

Theresa looks at Bonnie, feeling nervous because she knows Christine doesn't know how to give a good response under pressure. She awaits Christine's response.

"Well, we did talk to her recently. Heavenly is a survivor and a very smart girl. I know she's just upset right now, but she said she was safe," Christine says. She looks at Bonnie to see if she believed what she just told her.

"My concern is, if she is in danger she cannot warn you of her whereabouts. So you didn't call or you don't plan on calling the police?" Bonnie asks.

Christine looks at Theresa and then looks away. She keeps her head down as she says, "No, I didn't call the police."

Bonnie continues to write notes as she says, "Well, the good thing is you did speak to her. Do you plan on going back to your home or will you stay here?"

Christine responds, "I would like to go home, but I don't think me and the kids would be able to live there peacefully. I'm going to put it on the market; sell it and buy a new house with that money and the insurance money."

Bonnie continues to write notes. She wants to make sure she has all the information she needs. "So they did release the insurance money, which is good. Are you staying in New Orleans, or are you moving out of state?"

"Yes, they released the money about a week ago. I'm not moving out of state. That would be too much for my family."

Bonnie writes down Christine's response and says, "Well my session with the both of you is done. Can you let me speak with the children privately? I would like to get the phone number to Heavenly as well."

Theresa and Christine exit the kitchen and call Lindsey to speak with Bonnie.

"Hello, Lindsey. You are amazingly beautiful and growing so fast. How have you been?" Bonnie asks.

Lindsey replies, "Okay."

Bonnie doesn't want to upset Lindsey, but she needs to know if they have really talked to Heavenly. She has a strange feeling about Theresa's and Christine's reactions to Heavenly being missing. "Have you seen or spoken to Heavenly recently?" Bonnie asks.

Lindsey hesitates to respond at first, but when she does respond, she lights up. "Yes I did and she's coming back real soon. I can't wait until she comes back. We will be a family again."

Bonnie writes down Lindsey's response and her change in behavior when Heavenly was mentioned. "Is there anything you want to tell me? I see how excited you became when you spoke about Heavenly."

"No, I don't have nothing to say. Can I leave now?"

Bonnie sees in Lindsey's face that she is irritated so she agrees to let her leave. "Thank you, Lindsey. Yes, you can leave. Would you please do me a favor and send Mark to me?" Lindsey doesn't respond. She just gets up and walks away.

Mark walks slowly into the kitchen, seeming hesitant to see Bonnie. "Hi, Mark. Come have a seat. We won't be long," Bonnie says.

Mark plops down in the seat and looks at Bonnie. His stare is emotionless. "Hi," Mark says.

"How are you feeling today?" Bonnie asks.

"Good."

Bonnie notices he seems withdrawn and, as she remembers, he relies on Heavenly's permission to answer any questions, so she must have a strategy. "So, how are your sisters and your mom?"

"They're okay," Mark says.

She notices he is going with very short answers, so she is going to focus more on him. "So how are your new living arrangements going?" she asks.

"Good."

"Okay, well I am glad to hear you all are doing good. Have you talked to Heavenly or seen her lately?" Bonnie asks.

Mark begins to play with his hands as a sign that he is very uncomfortable. "I talked to her, but…" Mark says as he very easily shuts down and becomes very quiet. Bonnie notices he is very uninterested in a conversation with her, but he seems like he has something to say.

"Well, I am glad you spoke to her and I'm sure it made you happy. We're done talking unless you have something you want to tell me," Bonnie says.

Mark ignores her and just walks away without saying goodbye. Bonnie continues to write her notes from her visit with the family. She also makes a note to give Detective Jean a call, as the family's behavior toward Heavenly's sudden disappearance seems really awkward.

Bonnie walks toward the living room and she notices Theresa and Christine having a conversation. It is obviously a private conversation because when Bonnie gets closer to them, they cut the conversation short.

"Well, ladies, I hope I wasn't interrupting anything important, but I am all done here. I just need the contact number for Heavenly and I will be all set until you receive my decision," Bonnie says. She has her pen and pad in hand, waiting for one of them to respond.

"Thank you for coming to check on us. You weren't interrupting anything important. Let me get my phone and I will gladly give you the number. Maybe you can convince her to come home sooner," Christine says. She gets up and walks toward the kitchen to get her phone. Christine picks up the phone and as she opens it up to unlock it, she notices there is a media message from Heavenly. She looks around the corner to see what Bonnie is doing before opening the text message. To Christine's surprise, Bonnie is content in a conversation with Theresa.

Christine can't see clearly what the message is, so she taps the download button and waits for it to upload. Christine waits patiently. She is hoping for the best when she opens up the media message. Maybe Heavenly sent the family a loving video to tell them she is coming home soon. The video finally uploads, but it seems a little blurry so Christine takes a deep breath and with a smile on her face, she presses play. The contents of the video begin to play. Christine looks closer at the video, barely hearing any sound. Her heart beats fast, but what she is seeing has not completely registered yet. Studying the video again, her eyes widen as she becomes sick to her stomach. She places her hand over her mouth to prevent herself from vomiting. Then she screams out loud, "No, not my baby." The phone drops to the floor as she begins to cry and vomit on the floor.

Everyone comes to the kitchen to see what is going on. "What's wrong?" Theresa asks as she tries to comfort Christine.

As she is bent over releasing the contents of her stomach, Christine notices that Bonnie is standing there amongst her family. She is at a loss for words. Every time she tries to say something, the image of the video makes her sick to the stomach.

"I see Christine is not feeling well. Is there anything I can do?" Bonnie asks.

Theresa replies, "No, thank you. I will make sure I take care of her." She walks Bonnie to the door so she can hurry back to Christine.

"Call me and leave Heavenly's number on my voicemail if I'm not available. I hope she feels better and I will be in touch," Bonnie says as she exits the home.

Theresa runs back to Christine and says, "What kind of stupid stunt was that? You want this bitch to take your damn kids?" She stands and waits for Christine's response as she notices Lindsey and Mark standing quietly looking at the both of them. "Listen, go in the family room and watch TV. I will take care of your mother. She will be just fine," Theresa says.

They both look at her confused, but they leave the kitchen as she has asked them to. Christine mumbles something in between the release of her stomach contents. "Heavenly." She can't say it out loud or very clearly, between vomiting and her constant tears. She decides to point at the phone, as no one had noticed the video playing through all that had transpired.

Theresa walks around Christine carefully and picks up the phone. The video has come to a stop. Theresa totally blocks out Christine as her focus is now on this video. She presses play and the contents of the video begin to be exposed. Theresa tilts her head to the side as she tries to register the images she sees. As she continues to watch, she clearly recognizes the two people in the video.

"This motherfucker gotta die. What the fuck is he doing?" she says. She throws the phone at the wall and then goes to Christine. "Sis, I'm so sorry. I didn't know anything about this, you gotta believe me."

Christine pulls herself together and says with a saddened heart, "That's Reggie fucking my baby. What has your selfish ass done? Where the hell is my baby? Why the fuck is she with Reggie? You know what's going on. This has to be about you. He don't have no beef with me or my family."

Theresa stands there, lost for words as Christine approaches her and says, "Bitch, find my baby. I don't give a fuck how much money you got to spend. If you don't find my baby, they going to find you!" Christine heads to the kitchen to go clean up and get her thoughts together.

Theresa runs to get her phone and she dials a number. "Hello, meet me at the spot right now. This dude done violated, he fucked my niece and sent that shit to Christine. I'm on my way out the door right now."

Theresa hangs up the phone. She checks her purse to make sure all the money is there. She runs to grab her phone as it suddenly starts to ring. She looks at the number and doesn't recognize it. She hesitates to answer, but it could be important so she picks it up. "Hello," she says.

"Well, hello lovely lady," Richard says.

"Listen, I am very busy right now, Richard. I don't have much time."

Richard replies, "Are you sitting down? Because I have some information on Reggie and his family."

Theresa drops her purse and keys as she stands still to listen to what Richard has to say.

"You will be happy to know I found his family in Florida. He wasn't there, but his two children, his girlfriend, and her mother were. Her mother was nice enough to give me his number, so I can give you all the information now if you're ready. So your cousin is alive and well. Isn't that great news?"

Theresa nonchalantly replies, "Why, yes it is, Richard. Let me get a pen and paper. Go ahead."

Richard gives her the Florida address and Reggie's phone number.

"Thank you. I knew you could get the job done with good results. When you return, I will get with you for the rest of your payment," Theresa says.

Richard agrees and they both hang up, disconnecting the call. Theresa puts the information in her pocket, picks up her purse and keys, and she rushes out of the house to meet Low.

Lust

Father, have you forsaken me, or have my eyes deceived me?

You said I was wonderfully and beautifully made, but I can't see it. I just feel made.

I look at me and try to find you, but I guess my soul hasn't let you pass through.

As I fight with myself to hear your voice, I just keep acting like I made the right choice.

Until one day I open my eyes full of pain and that human being doesn't look at me the same.

Now I feel defeated, lost, and confused, but full of lust. As I fight with these emotions, I just want to be touched.

Not your touch, Father, because I never felt that, but the touch that makes my arch fall back.

This is all I know – that everyone loves. But what about the love from heaven above?

Do I pray now, or wait until later? Because this terrible feeling of lust and rejection makes me tell everything and everyone: see you later.

As I sit here and think of how I got here, I realized that it was the fear of love that let lust stay here.

~Champagne